For
Darryl + Jane
may the Bluebird of Happiness
splosh a load of it on
your doorstop.

Fond regards

The *Bitch* File

Enjoy

Robert F. Mager

Bob Mager

The Bitch File

Layout design and technical editing by Eileen Mager. Cover page design by Tony Amato, amato image Design, Inc.

Printed in the United States of America
ISBN-13: 978-1467938631
ISBN-10: 1467938637

Novels by Robert F. Mager

Killer in Our Midst

Dying for Jade

The Reluctant Miracle Man

The Price of a Miracle

Pursuing the Steamy Novel

Shen: The Chronicles of Madame Woo

The Bitch File

**Mager novels are available
from
Amazon.com**

Helping Minds

Unless you listen to the reactions of your intended readers, you may never learn what may have prevented them from picking up, and reading, your book.

To help locate my literary speed-bumps before, rather than after, publication, several generous people were cajoled into offering their valuable time to identify features that might have stopped them, turned them off, or somehow rubbed them the wrong way.

These generous folks must be revealed to posterity: David Cram, Margaret Fox, Dan Raymond, Sandra Krisch, Dick Koessler, Patty Schiano, Richard Ham, and Stephanie Jackson. Each contributed valuable feedback resulting in a more coherent and readable product.

Special thanks also to Rodney L. Cron, for sharing his valuable wisdom and encouragement, and for his welcome guidance through the bewildering swamp of the "rules" of fiction.

The indispensable editing was provided by Eileen Mager, who splattered many well-deserved marks on my "final" draft—thrice—while providing continual emotional support.

The cover was created by genius Tony Amato, Amato Image Design, who can turn an accidental ink splotch into a work of art.

As always, errors and omissions are the fault of my indigent computer, Glitch.

— *Robert F. Mager*

Chapter One

"Eeeee-yaahhh!" Bonnie Pentera shouted, her roundhouse kick slashing past the mid-section of her best friend, Angela Fortenza. The two women panted through another twice-weekly martial arts practice session on Bonnie's back lawn.

Angela leaped back barely in time to avoid serious damage to her ribs. "Yikes! Good work. Next week I'm gonna wear armor."

"Thanks, friend. But ... I'm bushed. How about ... we rest awhile ... do a few leg stretches ... and cool down?"

"Great idea. I've about had it, too."

Bonnie toweled the perspiration from her face. Still breathing hard, she continued. "There's something I want to run by you, Angela, and this might be a good time to do it."

"Okay. What's up?"

"A sticky situation, that's what. It ought not to be happening, but it is—and I'm having trouble figuring out what to do about it. If it continues, it could have serious consequences, both for me and my client."

The look on Bonnie's face told Angela it was time to shut up and listen.

"To begin, six months ago my consulting firm landed a contract at Marsden Manufacturing. It's a big project for us—and its success is critically important to Marsden as well—so I've put myself personally in charge."

"But?"

"But management has just done something so stupid it could cause the entire project to crash and burn."

"That does sound serious. What's it all about?"

"Okay, it's like this. At the moment, Marsden is making hi-tech parts and systems, mostly for the airlines and the military. Successfully so. But now they've signed contracts to manufacture a sophisticated line of high-tech *consumer* products aimed at a world-wide market."

"So what's the problem?"

"The consumer market is a whole new ball game for them. To make it work they'll have to retrain their sales staff—worldwide—to sell into a totally different kind of market."

"I ask again—what's the problem?"

"Well, since Marsden is almost ready to start the production lines rolling, it means the retraining needs to happen *before* the new products are ready for delivery. That means the new training program has to be developed, tested, and revised before being ready to put on line. In other words, that means they've pretty much got to get it done overnight."

"Ouch."

"Yes, ouch. Fortunately, management knows 'overnight' isn't realistic, but when they read my proposal describing how our technology can get the job done faster and better than they expected, they decided to take a chance on us. As a result, we landed the contract."

"Knowing how you work, I'm sure you'll get it done in plenty of time. So what's the 'stupid thing' management did?

"A month ago, they suddenly assigned a sales whiz name of Bartley Skeeg to head the Training Department. So now, because we're independent contractors working on their turf, we have to re-port directly to him."

"And that's bad?"

"Big time. He doesn't know squat about the training business, state-of-the-art or otherwise. Worse, he couldn't care less."

"Then why did they put him there?"

"I think they're trying to groom him for the Sales Manager's job. He's already a hot-shot *sales* guy, smooth enough to charm the skin off a snake, but there's a big difference between *selling* skills and *managing* skills."

"No kidding."

"Anyway, because management thinks Skeeg has potential, they parked him into this slot to give him a chance to learn the *managing* skills he'll need to qualify him for that position."

"Sounds generous."

"It is. But it's *wrong*. They want this guy to learn something about managing, but then they throw him into the deepest end of the pool by putting him in charge of a project he knows nothing about and which the company can't afford to have fail."

"Got it. Your project is high priority, but at the same time, management expects you to give this guy on-the-job training?"

"Yeah, something like that. But the thing is, this Skeeg guy isn't having any of it. He thinks the Training Manager job is a big demotion. He thinks since he's a hot-shot salesman he is *automatically* qualified to be *manager* of the sales force. That's his thinking."

"Dumb."

"But it's worse. You see, the other reason they put him there was to help me succeed with my project—share his expertise so we can teach it to others. Well, he isn't showing any interest in doing that, either."

"That's weird. No wonder you're concerned. So tell me about this guy."

"As I said, his name is Bartley Skeeg—"

"Skeeg? Strange name. Though that's hardly

his fault."

"You're right, but you may be dead-on about the 'strange' part."

"Your wrinkled nose tells me there's something more than meets the eye." Angela sat up and shook the grass from her black hair. "Come on—give."

"Okay. When I first met him I thought he was a real winner. You know, tall, good-looking, thick black hair, and a smooth talker."

"Sounds yummy."

"Yeah." Bonnie wrinkled her nose. "At first, I thought we'd develop a good working relationship. He was polite, articulate, and an experienced salesman. Should be a perfect match."

"But?"

"I discovered the yumminess is only skin deep."

"How so?"

"Well, when I found out he didn't know anything about what I was doing on his turf, I tried to get to know him better. After all, part of my job is to keep him informed about the project and I'm going to need his sales expertise to make it work."

"Sounds reasonable."

"I thought he'd be grateful for some input—most people are, in that situation." Bonnie sat cross-legged and continued toweling the dampness from her hair.

"So?"

"So, after he settled in for a few days, I invited him to a business lunch at a decent restaurant. Thought it would give me a chance to explain the project someplace where we wouldn't be interrupted. I was sure he'd want to know as much about what was going on in his new sandbox as possible. Well, big mistake."

"I smell a glitch."

"Yeah. I barely had a chance to tell him why our consulting firm was on his turf when the discussion turned from my project—ta da!—to Bartley Skeeg. From then on, it was all about *him*. All about his big scores as a salesman, and about how he'd been 'screwed over' by management's putting him in the Training Department instead of promoting him directly to Sales Manager. As I said, the company is trying to prepare him for bigger things, but he looks at it as a big demotion."

"Sounds like he was trying to sell himself to you," Angela offered.

"Exactly. It took everything I had to keep from smashing the blueberry pie right into his face. After he started talking about himself and his imagined slights, it was as though he'd turned into a different person. Not *once* did I get a chance to tell him anything about the project." Bonnie thumped the ground with a hand to emphasize the point. "I was completely flummoxed. I didn't know how to respond. I just sat there and nodded, as if I agreed with him."

"Well, you *did* say you wanted to—"

"I know, I *know*. I wanted to get to know him better, sure. But my purpose was for *him* to get to know the *project* better, too. Instead, I just wimped out and sat there listening passively to his egocentric monologue."

"I dunno," Angela said. "I think you're being too hard on yourself. After all, your mission was to get to know him better, and it sounds as though you accomplished it brilliantly."

Bonnie snorted. "I suppose you're right—when you put it that way. But it was humiliating, and I don't know what to do next. This guy is an enigma. One minute he's charming the pants off a client and the next, he's snarling at his secretary. I've got a critical project to lead and I need every-one chugging on all cylinders in the same direction to make it happen. I don't have time to baby-sit this guy, especially when he's not at all interested in learning anything new."

"So how can I help with—?"

She was interrupted by a loud, whiny buzz sounding from next door. As the sound grew loud-er, Bonnie's face darkened. As the whine in-creased in volume, a large remote-controlled mod-el helicopter popped above the basket-weave wall separating her yard from her neighbor, and hov-ered overhead, dancing about in the sky.

Bonnie's hands balled into fists of anger. "I swear I'm gonna *kill* that S.O.B."

"Who? Skeeg?"

"No, my idiot neighbor, *that's* who," Bonnie replied. "He flies that darned thing over there when I'm trying to do something in the yard, like soak up a few rays. *You've* been here before when it's happened. It's driving me nuts." She waved a fist at the hovering machine. "It's loud enough to curl the toes of the dead. I swear I can't imagine why the other neighbors put up with it. You'd think they'd have drawn and quartered him by now."

"Have you talked to him about it?"

"I've tried," Bonnie said, "but so far I haven't connected."

The noisy helicopter continued its dance, bowing, weaving, and occasionally dipping its nose in Bonnie's direction.

Angela laughed. "Looks like it's flirting with you. I think it's kinda cute."

"You *would!*" Bonnie leaped to her feet and ran for the garden hose coiled against the house. Turning on the water full blast, she ran toward the dipping mechanical bird and squeezed the nozzle's trigger, sending a stream of water over the fence to wash the nuisance from her sight.

The "bird," however, evaded her liquid "bullets," only to taunt her from another angle.

Keeping her eyes focused on her target, Bonnie ran straight for it to apply a killing stream. Completely absorbed in her mission, she failed to notice the coil of hose snagging her ankle. With a shriek, she tripped. When she dropped the hose, the nozzle turned back on itself and sprayed her from head to toe. Drenched, she stretched out her arms as she fell, convinced the hose had deliberately attacked her.

"Damn!" she said, examining her sore and stinging grass-stained hands. Spouting obscenities, wet, grass-stained, tear-streaked, face livid, she leaped up from the ground like an exploding rocket. "Now I'm *really* pissed!"

As if deciding it was time to retreat, the helicopter slowly settled out of sight.

Angela, now laughing so hard she could barely stand, staggered to the water faucet and turned it off.

"I am going to *kill* that guy," Bonnie said, clawing at the dripping blond hair covering her face. "He will rue the day he crossed blades with Bonnie Pentera." With that, she stomped toward the house. "And as for you—you *fink*—you can just stop laughing and remember you're supposed to be my best friend."

"Sorry," Angela said, struggling to keep a straight face.

Bonnie stomped into the house, through the kitchen and into the bathroom, dripping water with every step. Snatching a dry towel from its rack, she toweled herself vigorously. When the condition of her hair had improved from dripping

wet to merely damp, she stripped off her wet clothing and draped it over the tub. After scrubbing the
rest of her anatomy dry, she hurried to her bedroom. After donning dry clothing, she was ready
to do battle with her irritating neighbor.

"Are you in there?" Angela called from the
kitchen.

"Yes, I'm here," Bonnie replied. "Be right out."
True to her word, Bonnie appeared a moment later
and, grabbing Angela by the arm, propelled her toward the door.

"Hey, what gives?"

"I'm going next door to give that maniac a
piece of my mind, and you're coming with me."
The image of her pratfall and drenching still siz-
zled in her brain.

"Wait a minute," Angela complained. "Why
me?"

"I may need a witness in case I have to kill the
guy." Bonnie stormed toward the house next door,
dragging Angela by the hand.

"Are you sure you don't want to calm down a
little before you do something—"

"Never mind. Just come along and watch."

Striding to the back of the neighbor's house,
the two women found themselves face to face with
the offending helicopter. Next to it, screwdriver in
hand, stooped its master.

When he saw the two women coming toward
him, he immediately stood, brushed off his soiled

white T-shirt, and ran his fingers through his hair. None of which helped. His soiled clothing and smudged face masked whatever redeeming qualities might have been underneath. An unruly shock of hair bobbled on his forehead.

"Oh, hello," he said, smiling. "I wasn't expecting company." He picked up a rag and wiped his hands, but the look on his neighbor's face changed his mind about extending one in greeting.

"Hello yourself! I was hoping we'd never have to meet face to face, but I'm not about to put up with any more of your outrageous ... outrages." Bonnie caught herself sputtering.

The neighbor seemed taken aback by the unexpected outburst, but remained calm. "What outrageous outrage are you referring to, if I may ask?"

"You know very well what outrage!   It's that stupid helicopter ... *that* outrage. Invasion of my privacy! ... *that* outrage! That noisy thing flying over my yard, especially when I'm trying to get a little sun. *That* outrage, too."

"I'm really very sorry," the man replied, calmly. "I didn't mean to upset you. Honest!"

This was not the response Bonnie expected. When she verbally attacked, she expected people to react, not counter with calm, sincere-sounding apologies. That pushed her off balance.

"Well," she said, "you *did*."

"Look, uh ..."

"Bonnie Pentera," Bonnie said. Pointing to

Angela, who was by now on her knees examining the helicopter, she added, "and that's my friend, Angela. And you are—"

"Ramsey Toolen—"

"Oh?" Angela interrupted, "I thought your name was *Buzz*."

"Buzz?" Ramsey echoed.

"That's what Bonnie calls you."

"*Angela!*" Bonnie said, forcefully. "That's enough."

"Hmm," Ramsey said, stroking his chin as if in thought. "'Buzz.' I kinda like it."

"It's because of that darned buzzing helicopter—"

"You mean Heli?"

"Heli?" Bonnie said. "Did you say *Heli?*"

"Yes."

"You mean that thing has a *name?*"

"Of course. When I'm talking to other hobbyists it's a lot easier to refer to him by name—"

"*Him?*" Bonnie exploded anew. "The thing is a *male?* Well, I guess that figures, doesn't it?"

"Well," Ramsey responded, a twinkle in his eye, "lots of inanimate objects are assigned genders, you know. Ships are referred to as 'she,' and cars and planes—"

"Then how come *this* beast is a male?" Bonnie wasn't about to let go of her anger easily, though holding onto it was getting more difficult by the minute. This calm, polite man simply didn't warrant the treatment he was being given, and she was beginning to feel embarrassed by continuing her attack.

"I'd rather not say at this time," Ramsey said.

"*At this time?*" Bonnie mimicked. "Then at what time *would* you be willing to say?"

"I'd just rather not talk about Heli's anatomy until I get to know you better," he said with a smile.

That'll be the day, Bonnie thought.

"Look at this, Bonnie," Angela called. "This is really cute." Angela had knelt beside the resting helicopter to caress its sleek red body. "This is a really big helicopter."

"Heli has a sixty-inch rotor span. That's a fair size, but there are larger machines around."

"Not in *this* neighborhood, I hope." Bonnie wasn't about to miss an opportunity to vent what little remained of her anger.

"Hey, what's this thing?" Angela pointed to a small pod on the underside of the fuselage.

Ramsey walked toward Angela, Bonnie following close behind with fists still clenched.

"Oh," he said, "That's ... uhh ... that's the camera."

"The *camera?*" Bonnie's disappearing anger instantly revived. "You mean to tell me you can see me through that thing?"

"Mmm. Well, yes, I suppose I could—if it were turned on." Ramsey had been hoping not to have to talk about the camera until better acquainted with his neighbor. But now the "secret" was out, he faced the issue head-on. "It's just a little forward-looking camera—"

"*Forward?* I'd say *voyeuristic* is more like it," Bonnie sneered.

Maintaining his calm, Ramsey said, "Forward-looking means it can only look toward its front at about a forty-five degree down angle. It can't look straight down, sideways, or toward its rear ... unless I reset it."

"But it can *see* me when I'm in my yard?"

"Um ... yes ... it can—"

"And it can see me when I'm outside trying to get some sun?"

"Uh, yes—"

"And just *why* does it invade my privacy to do that?"

"Believe me, it isn't intentional. It's just that periodically I have to test a new component or two, and it's a lot faster to fly it for a few minutes in the yard than to truck down to the airfield where I always do the longer test flights. Besides, the camera is only turned on when I'm making lens adjustments, about once a month. Heli doesn't mind being blind most of the time—"

"You are ... one ... anthropomorphic *nutcase!* I suppose you talk to your computer, too?" Bonnie said, more forcefully than she'd intended.

"You mean Bugs? Of course. Don't you?"

"I cuss at it," Bonnie confessed, "But I don't *talk* to it."

"What *do* you talk to?"

"*Fang*," she blurted, before she could stop herself.

"Fang?" An amused smile crept across Ramsey's lips.

"Uh, my pet parakeet." Hurriedly, she added, "At least it's *alive*." Bonnie realized the shakiness of her logic, but was in no mood to debate the issue. "Don't try to change the subject."

"I wouldn't think of it. Look, Miss Pentera, I realize Heli is pretty loud and irritating. But that's only temporary. If you'll allow me, I'd like to show you what I'm trying to do about that."

"Like *burn* it?"

Ramsey ignored the jab. "I've got some other planes in my workshop downstairs in various states of disassembly. I'd be happy to show you what makes them tick, and how I'm planning to quiet them."

"Oh," Angela said enthusiastically. "I'd *love* to see what they look like on the inside. Let's do it, Bonnie. Please?"

Bonnie ignored her plea and turned to Ramsey.

"Did you say 'downstairs'?"

"Yes. Unusual for Phoenix, I know, but this house has a full basement. It was built during the seventies, I believe. Actually, it's the main reason I bought it. Great place to keep my toys."

In spite of her protestations, Bonnie's anger had worn off and she now felt a twinge of curiosity.

"Aw, c'mon, Bonnie. Let's do it. Please? I'd love to see his workshop."

"I promise you'll be perfectly safe," Buzz offered. "These are only airplanes, after all, not etchings."

"C'mon, Bonnie. Let's do it."

Bonnie, hands on hips, glared at Angela. "Whose side are you on?"

Chapter Two

Ramsey unlocked the cellar door and, with the flick of a single switch, flooded the entire basement with incandescent light.

Bonnie sniffed. "Don't you know that fluorescent lights would use a lot less electricity?" Still itching for a fight, her thoughts were interrupted by the man's eagerness to show off his toys.

"Let me give you a quick tour." Pointing to one corner of the basement, he said, "This is the supply room."

Both Bonnie and Angela laughed. The area indicated was more like a large bin into which discarded pieces of sheet metal, tubing, Styrofoam balls, and a hundred other oddments had been tossed.

"Go ahead and laugh," Ramsey said, "but I can find almost anything I need in that pile of junk. Moving right along," he pointed toward another area strewn with machinery. "This is my machine shop. Here, I can make just about any kind of part I need."

"Ooh, what's *this?*" Angela asked, pointing at a smallish machine bolted to a metal stand.

"A jeweler's lathe."

"Looks like the baby of this other one." Angela pointed to the large machine next to it."

Ramsey smiled. "You could say that. The bigger one is a full-sized metal lathe. That one over there is a vertical drill press, and that other one is a brake."

"A what?" The strange term intrigued Bonnie.

"A brake. Used for bending metal. And no, I have no idea why it's called a brake." After describing the machines' purposes, he walked toward a door on the other side of the basement area. As they turned to follow him, both women noticed some rings hanging from the ceiling.

"What the heck are those for?" Angela asked.

The rings, mounted approximately three feet apart, hung by short chains from the ceiling. They followed a path from the basement stairs, to the door toward which Ramsey was heading.

"Those are gymnast's rings," he said. "I don't like to exercise much, but I know I need it. So, when I come down to work, I swing my way from the stairs to the workshop on the rings. Gives me a good upper-body workout." Bonnie looked at Angela, trying to picture the scene. Unsuccessfully.

"Would you show us how it works?" Angela asked.

"Sure." Ramsey leaped up and grabbed one of

the rings, then swung easily from ring to ring toward his workshop door. Neither woman could keep her eyes off the bulging muscles rippling under his T-shirt as he swung from ring to ring.

"Amazing," Angela said. "What do you do about your lower body?"

"*Angela,*" Bonnie admonished. "I'm sure Mr. Toolen—"

"Just plain Ram will do ... or Buzz, if you prefer." The speech was accompanied by a smile.

"I like it," Angela said. "Buzz, it is."

"I'm sure Mr. Toolen has better things to do than—" Bonnie said.

"No, it's okay. Really. I have a special machine upstairs for exercising my lower body," he said. "It's a bicycle-powered computer."

"A what?" Bonnie found her curiosity about the man growing.

"I like to play computer games once in a while, so I fixed up a small generator and attached it to a stationary bicycle. When I pedal fast enough, the computer turns itself on and I can play while I pedal. No pedaling, no electricity. No electricity, no games. Keeps me pumping."

"Ingenious," Angela said. "So you get all the exercise you need without leaving home?"

"Right. It's like putting your refrigerator in the attic. The bigger your appetite, the more exercise you'd get running up and down the stairs." Ramsey opened the door to his workshop and

ushered his visitors inside. "This is where I actually build the planes. It's a separate room to keep
down the sawdust and metal filings."

What a mess, Bonnie thought. *There's stuff
everywhere, and the place stinks! The term
"chaos" must have been invented for this guy. I
could never live like this.*

The workshop housed a number of projects in
various stages of completion. Model airplane fuse-
lages and spare parts lay scattered around the
benches, along with an assortment of rotor blades.
A large helicopter fuselage sat on a workbench in
the center of the room. Tool racks covered the
walls.

Bonnie wrinkled her nose at the unmistakable
odor of airplane dope.

"What's this one going to be?" Angela asked,
fondling the helicopter fuselage on the center
bench.

Buzz explained, "This is my stealth heli. My
passion right now is to invent or devise a super-
quiet heli—"

"I'll drink to that," Bonnie interrupted, then
quickly added, "*Wait* a minute! You mean if you
manage to do that, you'll be able to sneak that
thing into my yard without my even *hearing* it?"

Buzz laughed. "I suppose so. But I promise
I'll try to give this one better manners than Heli
has."

"Does this one have a name yet?" Angela

asked.

"Not yet. Care to offer a candidate?"

"*Voyeur!*" Bonnie said.

"Not bad."

"I was being sarcastic."

"I know. But it's still not bad."

"You send that thing to spy on me and I'll do more than try to wash it out of the sky."

"I promise I won't."

"Thank you."

"So how're you coming with your quest for quiet?" Angela asked.

"I'm so close to making a breakthrough, I can taste it." He was truly serious, as well as enthusiastic, about his mission. "I'm focusing on the engine at the moment. If I can quiet it down some, and then do something about the muffler, it should make a lot of difference."

For the next several minutes Bonnie and Angela listened politely to more talk about engines, light-weight sound-proofing materials, and rotor dynamics than they cared to. In truth, however, Bonnie found the total immersion in his work appealing.

Shaking herself out of her trance, she turned to Angela and said, "We really should go, Angela. We don't want to keep ... uh ... Buzz from his glue-sniffing."

Buzz knew it wasn't meant as a joke, but he laughed even so.

"Sorry if I've bored you to death, but I really did want to show you what I'm trying to do here. Tell you what," he said to Bonnie. "From now on, I'll try to schedule my test flights for when you're at work."

"Thanks. It would also help if you kept the thing in its cage on weekends, when I'm at home."

"I think I can do that," Ramsey said.

"Fine. I don't need another surprise attack like today's. I must have looked a real mess, soaked from head to foot."

"Would you like to see the video?" Buzz asked, risking re-igniting Bonnie's rage.

"*What?* No, I don't want to see the video, Mister Smartass—I want to burn it."

Angela found this exchange highly amusing, for which she earned a sizzling glare from Bonnie.

"You're right," Buzz said. "Just as soon as I can check the camera adjustments, I'll have Heli deliver it to your picnic table. Tomorrow soon enough?"

"Now would be better, but okay. Tomorrow, at the latest. I'll wear my raincoat, just in case." Bonnie led Angela toward the door.

Angela turned back. "Thanks for the tour."

"My pleasure. May I invite you both for lunch some day soon?"

"We'll think about it," Bonnie said, fantasizing a blue-faced Buzz holding his breath waiting and waiting—forever.

Chapter Three

Bonnie and Angela sat at her kitchen table enjoying a cup of freshly-brewed coffee. "Well, what did you think of that?"

"Interesting," Angela replied. "I think he's cute."

"You *would*," Bonnie snorted.

"No, really! You know, you stormed over there and started attacking him before he could even introduce himself, yet he just stood there politely and apologized. You could tell he was genuinely sorry you have a problem with Heli."

"Holy cow!" Bonnie said, "Now *you're* doing it."

"Doing what?"

"Making that damned helicopter human—that's what. You'd think from the way you talk it was flying itself."

"Okay, c'mon already. Admit he acted like a gentleman from your very first blast."

"Well ... maybe ..."

"And it was darned thoughtful of him to show

us his workshop and explain what he's trying to accomplish." Angela smiled and touched Bonnie's hand. "I really liked him."

"Okay, I'll *sell* him to you. How much'll you give me?"

"Come on, Bonnie, you know you warmed up to him ... once you got over your mad."

"I'm not sure. I kept getting the feeling he was laughing at me behind those blue eyes of his. And the clutter—the disarray in his shop really turned me off."

"Come on, Bonnie, you know perfectly well that a man's workshop is a junkyard in progress— his private castle, so to speak."

"More like a cave, you mean."

"Oh, give it a rest. It's Saturday afternoon. At least he doesn't spend his time couching in front of football games. He's active. He's creative, and good-looking. You saw those muscles."

"Yeah, I guess you're right. It's just that I was totally embarrassed when that hose drenched me. What really made me mad is knowing it was my fault for not looking where I was going."

"*That's* the Bonnie I like. I wonder if he's divorced," Angela said.

"How should *I* know? Today was the first time I've actually met the guy."

"Uh-huh. But there's something else about him, you know. At no time during our visit did I see him looking at your chest."

The comment took Bonnie by surprise. "So, as if I care."

"Pretty unusual for you, eh?"

It was *very* unusual, Bonnie mused. She'd endured teasing during her early years because of her ample bosom, which had grown to adult size by the time she reached the age of twelve. Adding insult to injury, her erect posture made it difficult to ignore. She countered by wearing baggy tops, which irritated her fashion sense no end.

As a result, Bonnie found it hard to establish a genuine relationship with a man; she believed, from experience, their only interest was in her boobs.

"It certainly is unusual, if true," Bonnie said, who found Angela's observation disturbing. On the one hand, she was resentful of men who seemed to see only her body, but now, she found herself distressed about meeting a man who didn't seem to notice her as a woman at all. Was he so pre-occupied with his darling machines he didn't even *see* the real live woman standing next to him?

Angie's next question startled her out of her reverie. "So are you going to take him up on his offer of lunch? You really should, you know."

"*Why* should I take him up on his offer, my dear Little Miss Matchmaker?"

"Oh, no good reason at all, except that he's good-looking, smart, active, has good manners, and—"

"*Enough* already. If it will get you off my back,
I'll promise to call him."

"When?"

"*Angela!*"

"Okay, okay. Peace. It's just that Buzz seems
like a diamond in the not-so-rough ... compared to
this Skeeg guy you were telling me about."

Bonnie's thoughts turned to Skeeg and his behavior during the lunch she'd so carefully arranged. Angela was right about her comparison of
Skeeg to Buzz. Compared to Buzz, Skeeg was a loser. Frowning, she said, "I'd hoped we were going
to make a good team. But now I'm not so sure."
She thought a moment about Skeeg's situation.
"He's one of those poor souls tapped on the shoulder one day and told he was going to be a Training
Manager—just because he was good at selling. As
though being good at one thing automatically
made someone good at something entirely different."

"Does that really happen a lot?" asked Angela.

"All the time."

"So what's your next move?"

"Well, I'm going to give him the benefit of the
doubt for now. He could be avoiding learning
what we do because my project has been assigned
to his turf without his approval and he can't do
anything to get rid of it. Or because I and most of
my associates are women.   Or, he could just be in-
secure because all of a sudden everyone around

him knows what they're doing, and *he* doesn't. So I'll be nice to him and see if that moves things in a positive direction."

"Sounds like a plan."

"Y'know, I think what rankles him most is being 'passed over' for the job of Sales Manager. He just can't seem to see the great opportunity the company has bestowed on him. I wonder what else is eating at him."

"Keep me posted." Angela glanced at her watch. "Look, it's getting late and Tony'll have a cow if I'm late for our dinner date. He's a stickler for punctuality. Same time next Tuesday?" Angela put her coffee cup in the sink and turned to go.

"Yup. Same time. Give my love to your cop-husband."

"All right, but how about we dress up kind of sexy next time we exercise, just in case Heli comes back to flirt?" Angela slipped quickly out the door, barely in time to avoid being drenched by the wet towel winging its way toward her head.

Chapter 4

The following morning, Court Nesbitt, Vice President of Human Resources at Marsden Manufacturing Company, stood at his desk reviewing the employment history of one Bartley Skeeg. At a knock on his open door, Nesbitt called out, "Come in, Bart. Have a seat." He waved toward the chairs in the corner.

Nesbitt's office was unusual. A stand-up desk stood in one corner, but no accompanying chair. When asked about this unusual preference, Nesbitt often explained, "Two reasons. First, standing at my desk helps my posture and gives me a little exercise. Second, it keeps meetings short. People coming to see me at my desk don't dawdle when they have to stand throughout the conversations."

A small glass-topped coffee table sat in one corner of the room, surrounded by three uphol-stered swivel-chairs. Those called to meet with Nesbitt quickly learned through the grapevine not to sit there without being invited. When Court Nesbitt invited you to sit, the meeting invariably had something to do with your future at Marsden Manufacturing.

Nesbitt placed a manila folder on the table and sat across from Skeeg. "Let's see, you've been in your new job about a month now." He consulted the folder. "How are things going?"

"Fine," Skeeg said. "Everything's humming right along."

"Getting details on the big picture?"

"Yes" Skeeg said. "I look in every day and read all the staff reports."

"Have you learned what they do?"

"Uh ... mostly, they run training courses," Skeeg said. "Well, sometimes they write the courses themselves, and sometimes they buy them from vendors."

Nesbitt cocked an eyebrow. Obviously, Skeeg hadn't learned much about the operation of the department during a month of opportunity.

"Bart, the corporate executives, from the CEO on down, are committed to implementing the latest in performance technology—"

Skeeg interrupted. "I thought I was supposed to be running a *training* department."

"That's my point," Nesbitt said. "In state-of-the-art companies it isn't just a *training* department anymore, it's more of a *performance* department. Surely you've learned at least that much during the time you've been on the job."

"Sure. Okay, we can call it that. No problem."

"I'm afraid I'm not making myself clear. They're called *performance* departments because they don't do business the way they did when training was their only service. Now, training is just one of the things they do to improve employee performance on the job. And *that,* Bart, means everyone in the department—especially you—has to get up to date.   We need desperately to be able to reap the benefits of the latest technology."

"Uh-huh," Skeeg said, nodding.

Nesbitt saw Skeeg's eyes glaze at his mention of the required learning. "Bonnie Pentera's project is going to play a key role in upgrading the skills of your department, which is ultimately expected to lead to significant improvement in the performance of everyone in the plant. By the way, how are you getting along with her?"

"Oh, fine ... I guess."

"What's your problem with her?" Nesbitt asked pointedly.

"Problem? I don't have any problem."

"I've heard you're not entirely satisfied with her work, that you don't think *any* woman belongs in your department. That true?"

"No, no." Skeeg paused before continuing. "I just don't think any woman should be reporting to *me* when she doesn't know the first thing about selling." He stopped short of admitting he was still sore that someone else was given the Sales Manager job, a point Nesbitt knew rankled Skeeg no end.

"I see. Well, let me be as plain as I can about this," Nesbitt said, ignoring Skeeg's faulty logic and leaning forward as he spoke. "Bonnie is an expert in performance improvement techniques. She needs expert input on selling from you so she can get the course content and performance measures right. That's the main reason we chose you, with your selling expertise, for this job. Another is that we're giving you an opportunity to show us that you'll be the right man for the Sales Manager's job, and even beyond. But mainly, we thought you'd be the ideal person to help propel the Pentera project."

"Uh, yeah. Thanks."

"Make no mistake, Bart. You *will* bring the department up to speed, and you *will* give Bonnie Pentera all the support she needs with the sales-revision project. Do I make myself clear?"

"Yes, sir."

"One final point. By your own admission, you know very little about training, and nothing at all about performance technology. If you want to succeed here, you'll remedy both those deficiencies pronto. We must have you on board, and producing. Or else. Clear?"

"Yes, sir." Skeeg obviously got the message, but his body language told Nesbitt it was clearly not to his liking.

Nesbitt was fully aware Skeeg didn't want any part of his present assignment and, especially, any part of Bonnie's project.

"I hope so. Your only chance to get the Sales Manager job you're thirsting for is to prove you can handle *this* assignment ... and do it well enough to make us sit up and take notice."

"Got it."

"Now, if you're open to suggestion, I have one that might help you succeed." When Skeeg nodded slightly, Nesbitt continued. "Bonnie is a real pro at what she does and can help you a lot. Consider her a great opportunity."

Another message Skeeg would rather not hear.

"If I were you, and if she is not otherwise committed," Nesbitt said, "I'd consider inviting Bonnie to the company's Fall Ball on Saturday. That will give you a chance to make a new start and get to know her better." Nesbitt had seen a couple of the floozies Skeeg consorted with; the presence of one of *them* at the Ball wouldn't do him the least bit of good.

"Bart, you're one of the best salesmen this company ever had, and ... well, let me just say I'd like to see you succeed at your present assignment." Nesbitt concluded with, "And do something about that chip on your shoulder. If your negative attitude toward professional women attracts a lawsuit, your career with this company will be over."

Chapter Five

Skeeg steamed all the way back to his office. The more he thought about Nesbitt's treatment of him, the more furious he became. Management obviously didn't know diddly squat about how to treat their star salesman. He was the best they had, and they'd tossed him aside like some piece of garbage. Well, he'd get even with 'em, one way or another, and he knew exactly how he'd start his campaign. He'd begin by charming the pants off everyone at that Fall Ball. With that Bonnie broad on his arm, he'd be the center of attention. He'd make 'em sit up and take notice.

Skeeg hustled into his office on the training floor, wearing a deep frown.

"Everything all right?" his secretary asked. "You don't look so good." Other secretaries in the organization were called "associates," but Skeeg preferred to call a spade a spade. In his mind, Brenda was his personal servant whose job was to do precisely what she was told.

"I'm fine," Skeeg nodded, brusquely. "I need

to talk to that Pentera woman. Get her into my office as soon as you can."

"I'll call her right away."

"Good." Skeeg headed into his office.

When Bonnie knocked on his open door and entered a few minutes later, she found Skeeg sitting stiffly erect behind his desk poring over one of her reports.

"Bonnie," he began, without asking her to sit, "I just had a long talk with Court Nesbitt, the Human Resources VP."

"Yes, I know who he is."

"Well, he reminded me that the company's annual Fall Ball is coming up Saturday night. He told me I should take you along. Okay?"

"Okay, what? Is that supposed to be an invitation?"

"Of course. It's formal, you know."

"So I've heard."

"So you'll come with me? It could do you some good."

"This can be characterized as a business meeting, right?"

"What do you mean?" he asked.

"I'll accept your invitation—if that was an invitation—but only with the understanding that this will be considered solely a company function—not a date."

"We'll consider it any way you want."

"All right. Then thanks for the invitation. I've

heard these Fall Balls are rather elegant." She was anxious to attend, but would much rather be escorted by someone else—*anyone* else.

"Yeah. They pull out all the stops. One more thing," added Skeeg. "Be sure to wear something sexy."

"*Why?*" Bonnie bristled.

Skeeg didn't expect this response, and didn't know how to respond. "Well ..." he stammered, "it'll help us make points with management."

"Uh-huh," Bonnie replied, shaking her head at his lame explanation.

"I'll pick you up at six."

*   *   *

Bonnie phoned Angela as soon as she arrived home that evening.

"It's me," she said, when Angela answered.

"What's happening?"

"I had a pretty strange day and I need to bounce it off you. Got a few minutes?"

"Sure. Tony won't be home for a couple of hours yet. Want me to come over?"

"Uh, no. I've a bunch of work to do and I don't want to give myself any excuses to goof off. Let's just talk for a few minutes."

"Sure. What's up?"

"Well, every year the company hosts a Fall Ball at the Hyatt downtown. It's a big event—formal."

"And?"

"And Skeeg calls me into his office this afternoon to tell me the VP suggested he take *me* to the Fall Ball."

"Did he invite you?" asked Angela.

"Telling me the VP told him to take me. *That* was the invitation. This guy's got to be the most insensitive jerk I've had to do business with in a long time."

"Ouch. Maybe he thought he was being romantic."

"Romantic, my ass. He's about as romantic as a rutting hog. But that wasn't all. After insulting me with his so-called invitation, he told me to wear something sexy."

"He must think since he's your client, he can treat you like a servant."

"I don't know what he's thinking, except that if he's thinking what I think he's thinking, it won't do him any good."

"Did you say you'd go?" Angela asked.

"Yes, and I agreed to let him pick me up."

"What's wrong with that?"

"I don't want him coming to the house. I should have told him I'd meet him at the hotel."

"Can't you still change the arrangement?"

"I suppose so. But I know he's just using me to get attention for himself. If I changed the arrangements now, well, he already knows where I live. Now my problem is in figuring out what to wear."

"Why is that a problem?"

"Because I've only got one formal to my name."

"How many were you planning on wearing?"

"Oh, come on. You know what I mean. I must have been dreaming when I bought this dress."

"What's wrong with it?"

"Nothing is wrong with it. It's just that its low-cut and fits me like a second skin."

"Like I said, what's wrong with it?"

"It makes me look sexy as hell, and all the guys will just stare at my chest."

"This may come as a surprise to you, my friend, but you're not the only beautiful woman with gorgeous boobs."

"Angie, this is a business affair, and I don't want to come across like a temptress. If all the wives are more conservatively dressed, they may think I'm—"

"But you said the affair was formal, didn't you?"

"Yes, it is."

"Then the other women will be in formals, too. Right?"

"I guess."

"So, if all the women are wearing formals, how can you worry about not being conservative enough?"

"Well, maybe you're right. It's just that—well,

I'll feel sort of exposed."

"Ah," Angela said, "now I get it. You think that if you don't wear one of your bags—"

"*Angela!*"

"Well, it's true, you know. You've told me more than once how you hide your boobs with baggy clothes because you got all that teasing and whistles when you were a kid."

"All right, already! Knock it off. If it'll make you feel better, I'll wear the red dress. If it turns out to be the wrong thing, it'll be on your head!"

Angela chuckled. "Want me to promise to kill myself if you're the only one not wearing a bag?"

"Some friend *you* turned out to be." Bonnie had been lusting for an opportunity to wear her sexy dress. She just didn't want to have to wear it to a social event with Skeeg.

"Sorry. But hey, I'll come over Sunday morning to find out all about it. Don't forget a single detail. And, by the way, what do you hear from Buzz?"

"Nothing, thank you very much."

"No helicopters?"

"Not since I gave him a piece of my mind."

"There could be a message in that."

Chapter Six

Bonnie began preparing for the Fall Ball well in advance of Skeeg's expected arrival. She wanted to be standing at the door, ready, when he arrived, to avoid letting him into the house. After finishing her makeup, she put on her red gown and studied herself in the mirror. Not bad, she thought, adjusting the spaghetti straps on her shoulders. Five feet eight, flat stomach, straight blond hair settling in a curl on her shoulders. Not bad at all. Yet, though she knew the other women would be dressed in formal gowns—or cocktail dresses—she was still apprehensive. Remembering the catcalls and teasing she'd endured during earlier years, she had a sudden vision of an evening filled with more of the same. "That's irrational," she said aloud to her mirror image, "and you can just stop it right now! These are *adults*, for God's sake."

As she made her way through the kitchen, she heard a car horn honking. Melodic, but a horn nonetheless.

"Don't tell me the rube is gonna just sit in his

car and expect me to come running," she said to Fang, her parakeet. She was right. Skeeg sat at the curb in his black BMW. "I don't believe it! Oh well—at least I won't have to let him into the house."

Taking one final glance in the hall mirror, she picked up her purse and wrap, and opened the door. "Take care of the house, Fang," she called, and don't let anybody steal anything." As she locked it behind her, she heard the unmistakable whine of a familiar helicopter rising from Buzz's front yard. Gaining altitude, it moved forward to hover some fifty feet away. Responding to a sudden impulse, Bonnie flipped a finger at the helicopter. Heli dipped its nose in reply. For a fleeting moment, she thought an evening with Buzz might be considerably less irritating than one with the oaf in the BMW.

When Skeeg saw Bonnie coming toward him, he hurriedly stepped out of his car, in time to see Bonnie's wave, and the answering salute.

"Somebody you know?" he asked.

"In a way." A small smile spread over her face. She didn't bother to elaborate.

"You are one beautiful babe, you know that? I bet I'll have the most gorgeous date at the Ball."

"It is *not* a date, remember?" Bonnie said, ice in her voice.

"Oh, right."

Skeeg must be impressed, Bonnie thought; *he*

actually walked around the car to open the door for me. He was dressed in a black tuxedo, with a pale blue tux shirt, and wore a dark blue tie. *My God,* she thought. *Those shirt studs look like real opals. I guess he went to some trouble, after all!* Skeeg shattered her dream when he froze, staring openly at her cleavage as she stooped to get in. *Oh well,* she thought, *guess I shouldn't have expected anything different.*

During their uneventful ride to the hotel, Skeeg's monologue recounted his great sales, sprinkled with the "big names" to whom he planned to introduce Bonnie during the evening.

Skeeg eased to the curb at the Hyatt, climbed out of the car to make valet arrangements, leaving Bonnie to fend for herself. Once he had the parking claim check, he escorted her inside.

"Looks like everybody is gonna be here tonight," Skeeg said. He searched the lobby for someone important to whom he could introduce his spectacularly sexy date. Seeing no one who interested him, he ushered Bonnie toward the lobby-floor ballroom, where the sounds of lively music swelled as they entered.

"It looks as though the company's spared no expense," Bonnie said, noting the bright red, yellow, and purple floral decorations hanging from the walls and ceiling, and the bouquets of flowers decorating every table. Leaning over the nearest table, she sniffed, "Just get a whiff of these gor-

geous roses—and gardenias. The entire ballroom
is alive with their fragrance."

"Yeah," Skeeg said. "The company always goes
all out for the Fall Ball. They focus on different
themes, but always use that same silver ball."
Skeeg pointed to the rotating ball of mirrors bath-
ing the hall in darting shafts of colored light.

Bonnie asked, "So what's this year's theme?"

"I don't have a clue," Skeeg replied.

You can say that again, Bonnie thought.

A white-jacketed usher led them to a table
some distance from the dance floor. Skeeg quickly
walked around the table to check the names on the
place cards, hoping they'd been seated with someone important. He seemed disappointed to note
the remaining six places were assigned to three of
his department staff and their spouses. Scanning
the room for persons worth talking to, Skeeg noticed the location of the bar.

"I'm gonna get a drink. Ya want one?"

"White wine, please." *Oooh,* she thought, *his
impeccable manners leave me breathless. How in
the world can he be such a successful salesman
when he's with customers, and such an ass when
he's not?*

While Bonnie welcomed the other couples arriving at their table, Skeeg wandered off to collect
the drinks. The trainers introduced her to their
husbands, or wives, who looked at her with obvious—but thankfully not at all rude—appreciation.

The husbands then wandered off to forage for drinks at the bar.

Skeeg had stopped several times to talk with various people on his way back from the bar. It seemed to Bonnie it took forever before he delivered the small glass of wine. After sipping their libations, Skeeg nodded to the others at the table, and quickly began leading Bonnie toward the other end of the hall.

"Come on, there's some people I want you to meet," he said. "A couple of vice presidents and the manufacturing manager. They're good people to know." Skeeg led Bonnie through the banquet hall in the direction of his quarry. A number of heads turned to stare as they passed. When they approached the first of Skeeg's targets, they waited politely until their presence was noted.

"Mr. Cardoza," Skeeg said, "I'd like you to meet Bonnie Pentera. Turning to Bonnie, he said, "Mr. Cardoza is Vice President of Finance."

"How do you do," Cardoza said, bowing slightly.

"I'm pleased to meet you." Bonnie smiled, genuinely interested in knowing more about this handsome man with the bushy black hair.

"Actually," Cardoza said to Skeeg, "I know all about Ms. Pentera."

"You do?" Skeeg had surprise written all over his face.

"Yes, indeed. I recently had occasion to review

the history of her project, and the reason it was initiated. And," he said, turning directly toward Bonnie, "I'm very much looking forward to your report of the program tryouts."

"Thank you," Bonnie said. "I think you'll be pleased."

"Splendid," Cardoza replied.

Irritated at being left out of the conversation, and at the attention paid Bonnie by this executive, Skeeg tugged at Bonnie's arm. "I see someone else you should meet," he said.

An embarrassed Bonnie quickly excused herself from Cardoza and followed Skeeg toward his next target.

"Pardon me, Miss Bourneux," Skeeg said to an attractive woman in her mid-fifties—and mispronouncing her name as "Bornux." "Miss Bourneux, I'd like you to meet Bonnie Pentera. She's doing a project for me in the Training Department." Then, turning to Bonnie, he said, "This is Miss Bourneux. She's Vice President for International Operations."

"Delighted to meet you," Bonnie said. "I've been following your articles in *Connections*; I'm really impressed with your analysis of why the EU is likely to fail." *Connections* was the internal monthly newsletter distributed by the International Division.

"Really? It's nice to know someone actually reads it. But you know, those gargantuan unfunded pension obligations really are the ticking time bomb." With that, the two women entered into an informed discussion of European prospects, again leaving Skeeg standing mutely between them. He had no idea what they were talking about.

By now, Bonnie recognized from Skeeg's silent, uncomprehending stare, that he was definitely jealous of the attention she was receiving from the "top brass." Even so, though he knew nothing about the topics being discussed, just standing near the center of attention seemed to excite him. He tried turning the situation to his advantage.

"Excuse me," Skeeg said, "I believe dinner is about to be served and I'd like to introduce my girlfriend here to one or two people before we sit down."

"Of course. I quite understand."

Bonnie's suddenly rigid body, reddening cheeks, and blazing eyes made it obvious to everyone nearby that Skeeg had blundered in a big way by referring to Bonnie as his girlfriend. It was also obvious to everyone why Skeeg had been rejected as a candidate for promotion to Sales Manager. What was not obvious was how he had managed to rack up a successful sales record. Maybe because most of his clients had been men? Or, maybe he saved his charm for clients, and saw co-workers as not worth the trouble?

Bonnie, incensed at Skeeg's reference to her as his girlfriend, told him so as soon as they moved out of earshot. "I *definitely* didn't appreciate your referring to me as your girlfriend, Bart. You know perfectly well there's nothing between us, and I'd appreciate it if you'd knock off that kind of talk. It's embarrassing."

"Aw, come on," Skeeg said. "Lighten up. I was just making polite conversation."

"You were making conversation, all right, but it definitely wasn't polite. And don't you think it's a little hypocritical to refer to me as your girlfriend in view of your negative feelings about me and my project?"

"What?" Skeeg appeared surprised at the sudden hardness in Bonnie's voice. "Well," he said, as they made their way back to their table, "I admit I'm not too keen on having people who don't know anything about selling trying to develop sales courses. But that doesn't have anything to do with *you*."

"It has everything to do with me." *The gall of this man!* But before she had a chance to explore this bizarre turn of events further, they arrived at their table just as the salad was being served.

The dinner was pleasant enough, though table conversation was difficult due to the din caused by three hundred diners. Bonnie tried to steer the talk away from work, mainly so Skeeg wouldn't feel completely left out of it. She needn't have worried. No matter what they talked about, Skeeg managed to turn everything to his favorite subject: Skeeg.

When dessert was served—an obscene mound of mud pie drenched with dark chocolate—the harpist providing dinner music disappeared and the orchestra returned. Before long, dance music filled the room and Bonnie sensed a presence beside her. Looking up, she saw the smiling face of Mr. Cardoza.

"May I have the honor of this dance?" he asked, bowing slightly.

"I'd be delighted," Bonnie replied, rising to join him on the dance floor. *This is certainly going to be interesting, she thought. I wasn't expecting to be invited to dance by anyone, let alone a vice president. And such a handsome one at that!* Cardoza, who couldn't be more than forty years old, had a full head of shiny black hair, and skin that had seen a healthy share of sunlight. The cleft in his masculine jaw widened when he smiled.

"You're really a very good dancer," Bonnie said, as they glided expertly around the floor.

"Surprised that a number cruncher can keep his feet under control?"

Bonnie laughed. "No, it's just that I seldom think about the skills people might have that aren't work-related."

It was Cardoza's turn to laugh. "In that case, you'd be amazed at what some people do off campus. Why, I understand that some of them have weird hobbies. Even families and things."

"Touché," Bonnie said. Then, to change the

subject, "Does your wife know you asked me to dance?"

"*She's* the one who suggested it."

"But this is the first dance—"

"Ahh, yes, I see," Cardoza said. "I would of course dance with my wife, but I'm afraid she's traveling in a wheelchair."

"Oh, I'm terribly sorry."

"Thanks," Cardoza said, smiling. "But happily, it's only temporary. She broke an ankle on the tennis court, trying for a shot even God couldn't have made."

"I'm really glad to hear that—that it's temporary, I mean."

"Thank you. But there's something I wanted to talk to you about, and this seemed like a good opportunity."

Bonnie's curiosity instantly intensified, and her "Warning: this is business" sensors leaped to the alert.

"Tell me. Are the results of your first test of the new sales program as good as the grapevine claims?"

"Yes, they really are."

"Glad to hear it. We're in desperate need of a competent sales force that can handle our new consumer product lines. I'm afraid if we don't do something quickly, well, we're already heading for the tank."

The music stopped, and Bonnie turned to go

back to her table. Before she could thank him for
the dance, however, Cardoza took her gently by the
hand and guided her back toward the other waiting dancers.

"Please don't go just yet. There is one more
question I would like to ask you."

"Of course." The orchestra launched into its
next number, and the waiting couples resumed
dancing.

"This is somewhat delicate ... because it's none
of my business. Organizationally, that is. Don't
answer if you think my question indiscreet, but
much is riding on your perceptions."

Bonnie's curiosity antennae were now vibrating at maximum intensity. She nodded, and Cardoza continued.

"Is there any likelihood that Bartley Skeeg will
interfere with your project in any way?"

Bonnie had been expecting a question about
her personal life. "Uh ... may I ask what prompted
your question?"

"Let's just say I've heard Skeeg is behaving like
a sprinkle of sand in the gears of progress."

"To tell you the truth, he's only been on board
a few weeks and ... well, so far he hasn't learned
much about ... but I know he resents my project.
He's told me so. He thinks women who, in his
words, aren't 'hotshot salesmen,' should not be let
out of their cages, let alone be allowed to develop
sales programs when—to use his terms—'they

don't know squat about selling.' Yet—so far, at least—he hasn't interfered with the project."

"I'm glad to hear that. I'll hold those comments in confidence, of course. Now I want to tell you how serious the situation is, and ask you to hold *my* comments in confidence."

"Of course."

"The company is on far shakier ground than anyone realizes. The Board of Directors is seriously alarmed. They've been leaning on the executives to make things happen, and your project is at the top of their list. Without a top-notch international sales force, especially one that can sell the new consumer product line, we're dead. Am I scaring you?"

"Yes, very much so." Bonnie let her frown communicate her concern.

"Sorry, but here is what I would like to ask of you. If there is even the slightest hint that Skeeg is interfering with your project, I want you to contact me. *Me,* understand? Not Court Nesbitt, or anyone else." Cardoza reached into his jacket pocket and handed her a business card. "I've written my home phone number on the back. If you need to talk to me, use that number. And let's just keep this conversation to ourselves, shall we?"

"Yes, of course." Why, she wondered, would he ask her to call *him* if Skeeg misbehaved, instead of Nesbitt? Might he think Nesbitt wouldn't be able to act quickly or decisively enough, if action were needed? Maybe he had a lot of stock in the company and would take action himself, to minimize losses? Whatever the reason, Bonnie knew she'd have to be very careful about what she said, and to whom.

The music ended and Cardoza escorted Bonnie to her table. As they made their way through the crowd, Bonnie was struck by the realization that if Cardoza had *already* written his home phone number on his card before asking her to dance, it meant he had planned to talk to her during the Ball. If that were the case, the company situation must be serious indeed. *I wonder what he heard to make him suspicious of Skeeg.*

As soon as Cardoza thanked Bonnie for the dance and departed, Skeeg went on the attack. "Well, *that* took you long enough," he said, sarcasm dripping from his lips. "What were you two talking about all that time, anyhow?"

"None of your business," replied Bonnie, tersely.

"Well, I didn't think it was right that my date should be dragged off to the dance floor just as I was gonna ask her to dance." Skeeg's petulance triggered several knowing glances among the other diners at the table.

Bonnie's face flushed and her fists clenched. "I've asked you not to refer to me as your 'date'." Bonnie put enough ice in her voice to chill a bonfire. "You have no right to do so and I find it offensive."

The others stopped talking among themselves to listen.

Skeeg couldn't help noticing the stares. "Nothing to worry about, folks," he said. "Just a little lovers' quarrel."

Without a word, Bonnie rose from the table and strode toward the restroom.

"What'd I say?" Skeeg said, spreading his hands in a futile attempt at innocence.

In the restroom, Bonnie breathed deeply to calm her rage, then freshened her makeup while considering her options. Reluctantly, she decided her best course was to continue following her original plan. As she'd learned tonight, her project was even more important to the company than she'd imagined, and she had no desire to jeopardize its success. Therefore, she would continue to try getting along with the bastard, but from a distance, and only on the company campus. She didn't have to put up with his rudeness on her own time ... and she wouldn't.

But what to do about the remainder of the evening? She'd been looking forward to mingling with as many people as possible, and to dancing with a few of them. After Skeeg's boorish behavior, however, she wanted only to go home—and as soon as possible.

Leaving the restroom, she returned to the table to find Skeeg chatting with the only remaining couple. "Excuse me," Bonnie said. "I'm leaving."

"But you can't. It's still early. Don't you want to dance some more?" Skeeg whined.

"Yes, I do, but I'm even more interested in going home. No need to get up—I'll call a cab."

"Not a chance," he said. Reluctantly, he offered parting comments to the remaining couple, rolled his eyes, and ushered Bonnie to his car.

Chapter Seven

Once outside the hotel, Bonnie breathed the soft air of freedom. It was a balmy fall evening in Phoenix, but one she wished would soon be over. Though the lightest of breezes stirred, and its warm air calmed the soul, that condition existed only outside Skeeg's car. Inside, it was icy cold. They spoke little during the twenty-minute drive. Bonnie saw no sign of emotion in Skeeg, but there was no shortage of it in her, as she reran the evening's events in her mind and wondered anxiously about what the immediate future might bring.

Skeeg couldn't imagine what was *wrong* with Bonnie. He'd dated a lot of women damned *glad* to have him refer to them as his girlfriend. Even if she didn't want him to, what was the big deal? It wasn't as though he'd introduced her as his lover— or worse, his wife. But to put him down in public was going too far. *Oh, well,* he thought, *as soon as she calms down she'll come to her senses, then we can take up where we left off. By the time we get to her place she'll invite me in for a drink, and we'll spend a wild night in the sack.*

Bonnie also replayed the events in her mind. How could he be so unconcerned about her feelings as to ignore her repeated requests not to introduce her as his girlfriend or date? Did he actually believe they had some sort of relationship? If so, it must be based purely on her invitation to the business lunch, and possibly her acceptance of his invitation to the Ball. *Whatever drove this compulsion to think of me as his property will have to be stopped—now!*

As soon as Skeeg pulled to the curb in front of Bonnie's home, she quickly opened the door and stepped out.

"Wait a minute," Skeeg said, slamming out of the car and hurrying around to the curb side. "I'll at least walk you to your door."

"No need. I can manage." She speeded her walk toward her front door, fumbling for her house key.

Skeeg caught up just as Bonnie retrieved her key from her purse.

"How about inviting me in for a night cap? I can make up for whatever you think I did wrong tonight."

"No, thanks." Turning to face Skeeg, she added, "I'd just like you to say 'goodnight' and leave. Please."

"Come *on*," he said, angrily, moving closer, "You gotta give me *something* for the evening." He encircled her body with his right arm and, drawing her close, began pawing at her breast with his left. When he tried to force a kiss, Bonnie turned her head and slapped his hand away.

"*Stop* it," she commanded.

He persisted, trying to plant his lips on hers.

"Stop it!" she repeated, continuing to turn her head away from his searching mouth. "I said *NO*, and I *meant* it. Now *stop* it." She tried unsuccessfully to push him away.

Skeeg held her body tighter, his left hand tearing at the strap of Bonnie's low-cut dress. The strap broke. With a savage tug, Skeeg pulled the dress downward, along with the bra beneath it, exposing her breast.

The tinge of fear Bonnie had felt when the attack began escalated into near panic. She was now convinced he wasn't intending to stop until she gave in—if she didn't, he'd likely try to gain her submission by hurting her. She realized then she was actually being attacked!

As her self-defense mantra kicked in, her fear faded into the background. "I will *not* be a victim," the mantra commanded. "I will decide only how badly I want to hurt my attacker." In a flash, she weighed her options: End the attack, or disable her attacker long enough to get away and call the police. Bonnie made her decision.

Extending the fingers of her left hand, she jammed the "V" formed by her thumb and outstretched fingers firmly against Skeeg's windpipe. Simultaneously, she squeezed her thumb and fingers against the sides of his throat, blocking the blood supply to his brain.

Skeeg gagged and relaxed his hold, staggering backward to retain his balance.

Bonnie grabbed the thumb of his left hand. With the heel of her right hand providing leverage, she twisted his arm outward.

To ease the sudden pain, Skeeg dropped to one knee. Bonnie continued the pressure until Skeeg lay flat on his back. Following him down, she jammed a knee into his groin.

Skeeg screamed in pain and gasped for air at the same time. "I'll *get* you for this, you bitch," he wheezed, venom dripping from every word. He knew he was beaten. With his left arm painfully twisted, and a knee in his groin, he understood instinctively that his free right hand could do nothing to release him from Bonnie's powerful hold. Even if he'd had the will to do so, he didn't know how. His street-fighting days hadn't prepared him for a skilled adversary like Bonnie. He seethed with anger and frustration. Being beaten was humiliating enough—but to be beaten by a *woman!* That was more than any man should have to endure. "You'll be *sorry*," he said, vowing vengeance.

"If you promise to behave and leave immediately, I'll let you up," she said, maintaining the pressure on arm and groin.

"You're gonna regret this big time. Now get offa me."

"If you promise to go quietly, I promise not to report this attempted rape to the police.

"Whaddaya mean, attempted rape?" Skeeg whined. "I was just trying to give you a goodnight kiss."

"Sure," Bonnie said, "and that's why you pawed me and ripped my dress. If you promise to leave me and my project alone, I won't say anything about this episode to anyone at the company. Deal?"

Skeeg knew he was a "dead duck" if Bonnie recounted any part of the evening to even one person. The gossip would spread at the speed of light.

"Oh, okay," he promised, reluctantly. "Now let me up before you break my arm."

Bonnie released his hand. She kept her knee in his groin, however, until she was sure he wasn't going to renew his attack. She needn't have worried. Skeeg was much more interested in his painful crotch and bruised left arm, now massaging the arm with his right hand.

The fight over, Bonnie stood up and let Skeeg rise, while trying to cover her exposed breast by pulling up her bra and torn dress.

Without a word, Skeeg brushed himself off and, limping and bent over to ease the pain in his crotch, headed for his car. He slammed the car door shut and drove off, his wheels screaming his anger and frustration.

Chapter Eight

When Skeeg's car screeched out of sight, Bonnie's hands began to shake uncontrollably, and dizziness suddenly overwhelmed her. Holding her hands outstretched to avoid falling, she shuffled to the decorative stone bench beside her front door. Slumping to the bench and inhaling deeply, she lowered her head between her knees. After-action stress syndrome, she diagnosed, the reaction of someone surviving a life-threatening situation. *Jeesus, the nerve of that man!*

Suddenly sensing an approaching presence, her alarm bells rang anew. Trying to resume a state of alertness while still shaking, she pulled at her torn dress in an attempt to cover herself. Forcing her head erect, she turned to face the approaching presence, as her neighbor ran toward her.

"Are you all right?" he asked, dropping to one knee in front of her.

"Oh, it's you."

"Sorry." Buzz stopped abruptly and backed

away, spreading his hands in front of him. "I just thought you needed help."

"Sonuvabitch tried to *rape* me."

"Yes, I saw it."

"You *saw* it?" she said, surprised.

"I was looking out my living room window. But before I could get to the front door, you'd already made your moves and had him on the ground. That was a nice piece of work."

"Yeah. Well, the bastard deserved it."

"What stopped you from killing him?"

"Took the fight out of him, so I stopped." Still panting for breath, she continued. "Probably seventeen ways I could've killed him, though."

"Believe me, I *believe* you," Buzz said, in genuine admiration. "But are you okay? You're not hurt or anything?"

"No. I'm not hurt. Just shook up."

"Understandable," Buzz said. "Here. Let me help you up. I want you to come to my house." He offered his hand.

"*Why?*" a suddenly suspicious Bonnie asked. Flashing back to her childhood, she remembered how her military father had drilled her with the importance of self-reliance. Ever since, she considered leaning on someone else a sign of weakness.

"It's not likely, but 'lover-boy' just might come back. I don't want him finding you like this."

"Like what?"

"Shook up. Not at your best. The guy might decide to come back and escalate."

"Escalate?"

"He might have gone to get something with more wallop to attack you with. Mace, knife, gun, rope, you name it, these creeps will use it."

Looking directly at Buzz's face, she wondered how he had become so well informed in such matters. And why. But much as she disliked being dependent on anyone, she welcomed the offer of a helping hand. She let him lead her across the lawns and driveway separating their houses, to his front door.

When he ushered her in, she froze in surprise. The upstairs area didn't remotely resemble the disorder of the basement. Beautifully furnished, immaculate, in stark contrast with the "working dump" beneath it. In addition to the elegant furniture, a vintage player piano stood against one wall, an old juke box against another. Though from another era, the piano looked freshly-delivered from a showroom. Bonnie couldn't resist sliding an appreciative hand along the keyboard cover.

"This is fantastic!" she said, distracted from her distress. "Where'd you get it?"

"Just a little something I picked up along the road of life," he replied. "I'm an accomplished musician, you know," he said, a mischievous twinkle in his eye.

"No, I didn't know. What do you play?"

"Player pianos. I can play any player piano in existence."

Bonnie, realizing she'd been had, punched him lightly on the shoulder. Actually, she was grateful for the moment of levity; it helped to calm her. Holding her extended fingers in front of her face, she noted they barely trembled.

Buzz noticed. "It would help to take a few more deep breaths," he said, handing her a snifter of what smelled like brandy. "Here," he said, "take a swig of this while I get something more substantial than that lace to wrap around your shoulders."

"Thank you," Bonnie said. "I think I need this." She lifted the glass and downed a generous dollop.

"There's more when you're ready."

"You trying to get me drunk?"

"Of course," he replied. "I do that to all the beautiful women I meet."

Bonnie began to protest, but Buzz held up a hand. When he returned with a lightweight jacket, she slipped her arms into the offered garment. The torn bodice of her dress, no longer supported by Bonnie's hand, dropped to uncover a generous portion of her right breast, as well as the maroon bra barely holding it in place.

My God. My boob is practically waving in his face, and he hasn't even noticed.

"Thank you for the jacket. That was very gentlemanly."

"Would you like a small safety pin to help nail that strap in place 'til you get home?" he asked.

"If you have one. That would be very nice."

When Buzz left to retrieve a pin, Bonnie decided it might be a good idea to let him do the pinning. Her hands were still a bit shaky and she was beginning to feel the effects of the brandy. In that condition, she didn't trust herself with a pin. At least that was what she told herself. Though she wouldn't admit it, she was feeling a bit like an ugly duckling.

"Would you mind?" she asked, slipping the jacket from her shoulders. "I don't think I can reach the strap."

"Sure," he said. Reaching behind her for the loose strap, he placed it over her shoulder and, moving his head close to her body to better see what he was doing, deftly threaded the pin through strap and bodice.

"There," he said, standing again. "That ought to hold until you get home."

"Thank you," she said, softly, stunned. "Y'know," she said, "I thought you were an insensitive slob."

"Insensitive slob?" Buzz repeated, chuckling. "What have I done to deserve that?"

"You made your heli—helipopter get me all wet ... and then you showed me your messy basement."

"Oh. I guess those were good enough reasons.

And now?"

"Now I'm not so sure." The brandy, having dissolved much of her decorum, allowed her to kiss him lightly on the cheek.

"I am definitely going to have to buy another case of that brandy," Buzz said.

"And I'm definitely going to drink some of it," she replied.

"That was a very courageous thing for you to do, you know."

"What? You think I've never kissed anyone before?"

Buzz chuckled heartily. "No, I was referring to your decking the bad guy. I've never seen those moves executed more smoothly in my entire life. That guy never had a chance."

"Thank you," Bonnie said. "I was gonna kill him, but I didn't want to have to clean up the messy mess."

"Who is he, anyway?"

"My client at Marsden Manufacturing. My consulting company has a project going in his department and he's the guy I have to report to. Took me to the Company Fall Ball down at the Hyatt. Made an ass of himself and I made him bring me home early. When I wouldn't give him what he said I *owed* him for the evening, the jerk attacked me."

"Want me to call the police?"

"No, no. Please don't. I made a deal. I told

Mister Sleazeball that if he left me and my project alone, I wouldn't report him either to the police, or to anyone at the company."

"Think that's wise?" He reached out and touched her shoulder, pulling the jacket up over his handiwork.

Bonnie chuckled. "He's got a lot more to lose than I do. His job isn't very secure and I think he knows it. Anyway, tonight I learned my project is more important to the company than I'd realized. If he interferes in any way, he'll be gone in a minute." She tried unsuccessfully to snap her fingers. "Poof! Just like that."

"Got it. We'll begin taking steps right now. Wait here." Buzz headed for his basement workshop, leaving Bonnie to wonder what he'd meant by "we."

He returned a minute later and handed her a thick silver-dollar sized object.

"What's this? Another video camera?"

"No. It's a signaling device. Keep it with you when you're home—it's only good for a few blocks—press this little button if you need help. I'll come running."

Bonnie looked up from the gadget into Buzz's eyes, and saw concern. *My God, he wants to protect me!* She couldn't remember when a stranger had shown enough concern about her well-being to guard her from harm.

"What does it do?" she asked.

"If you need help, just press the button. Go ahead and press it now," he urged.

She did, and instantly loud alarm horns blared throughout the house and workshop.

"*Jeesus!*" she shouted, covering her ears. "Turn that thing *off.*"

Buzz ran to his study, disabled the alarm, and returned to Bonnie. "I can hear that from anywhere in the house."

"No kidding. I'll bet they can hear it anywhere in the neighborhood. How does it happen you even have such a thing ... all tuned up and ready to go?"

"A friend of mine and I invented it a few years ago. It was developed as a threat-warning device. It can be set to trigger horns like the ones you just heard, or make it energize a vibrating unit in your pocket."

The image of men walking around with vibrators buzzing in their pockets was too much. Bonnie started to laugh. *Ooh,* she thought, *I can build a brand new fantasy out of this.*

"What's so funny?" Buzz asked. "I'm serious—this thing really works."

"No question about that!" she said. "It's just that I got this picture of a bunch of men walking around with buzzing vibrators in their pockets." She laughed some more.

Pretending to be serious, Buzz said, "You know, you just may have something there. Why, with just a few adjustments I could—"

"Could what?" The snickers abated to mere sniffles.

"Make a commercial pocket vibrator activated by a button like this one. We could make millions," he said. "It was your idea, so we'd split the proceeds right down the middle. Know any good marketing people? I can see the billboards flashing. For now, though, I'd like you to keep this thing hidden on your person. Someplace you can get at it."

"Okay. Thank you. Will you come running even if I'm not being attacked?"

Buzz smiled. "It will be my honor. A lady in distress is a lady in distress."

"Y'know," she said, her voice growing more slurred, "You may be talking sense, but I don't think I'm listening sense."

"No problem. Can I ask you a serious question?"

"Ask away."

"What's going to happen when you go to work Monday?"

Bonnie frowned, trying to think through the fuzziness of the brandy. "What I hope will happen will be business as usual. I don't think Skeegy-boy will make any trouble ... not for a while, anyway. It'll take time for him to recover from my knee." She stumbled on to describe Skeeg's success as a salesman, and his insensitivity toward women.

"He's a Jerkyll—uh—Jekyll and a Hyde, all wrapped up in the same skin. Got the picture?"

"In spades." Buzz did indeed "get the picture" of Skeeg's true nature and didn't like what he saw. But this was no time to alert Bonnie to the potential danger of the situation. "Look, Bonnie. Call me if I can help in any way at all. You know I'm almost always here—"

"And that's another thing I've wondered about. Now that you're an ex-slobberino, I wanna ask you ... how come you don't *work* for a living?"

Buzz laughed. "Actually," he said, "I *do* work for a living. I just do most of it right here. I earn money trading investments on the Internet, and work on a few consulting projects here and there. Also, I have a research grant from the Pentagon that supports my work on the stealth helicopter project."

"Oh, yeah," Bonnie slurred. "*That* project. Ol' stealthy-wealthy. How's it coming?" Bonnie normally spaced her drinks much farther apart than she had tonight. But, then, being physically attacked was anything but normal.

"Better than expected," Buzz said, warming to his favorite subject. "I expect to finish a working prototype within a few days. If you promise not to bring your hose, we can fly it together."

Bonnie was surprised to hear herself saying, "You think there's room? I think I'd like that. And I'll leave hosy-wozy at home." As a silly afterthought, she waggled a finger at Buzz. "I'll just bring the nozzle. A girl needs *some* protection. Now I think I'd better go before I make a bigger fool of myself. I gotta go look in on Fang."

"Fang? Oh, yes, your pet gorilla."

"Parakeet."

"Sounds more like a pet gorilla. I'll walk you home."

Chapter Nine

Sunday morning arrived as an unwelcome event. Head throbbing, Bonnie's eyelids refused delivery on neural messages demanding they stay open. Signaling her body that a command to move would soon be arriving at all points, she closed her eyes in preparation for the ordeal. Ten minutes later, she stumbled out of bed. Accompanying that difficult maneuver with a variety of groans and sighs, she dragged herself unsteadily toward the source of coffee, and fumbled through the motions required to produce the desired steaming result.

Hot cup finally in hand, her mind focused on a long, leisurely soak. She headed for the bathroom, sipping her brew, each step accented by the entire percussion section of the Phoenix Symphony in her head. She felt a little more human after the caffeine trickled through her system, and even more so after inhaling the steam rising from the hot water filling her tub.

She carefully aimed her right foot toward the water to test its temperature while holding on to the grab bar. Just as the toe of her foot touched the water, the phone rang.

"Damn!" Lowering her leg to the floor, she propelled herself her to the cordless phone she'd left on the kitchen counter.

"Hullo."

"Hi. It's me," Angela said, much too brightly for one in Bonnie's condition.

"Please don't sound so cheerful, and why are you calling me in the middle of the night? And why are you shouting?"

"Uh-oh," Angela said. "Sounds like somebody had a night on the town."

"Not exactly."

"I want to hear all about it. Every detail."

"Angela, I was just about to plop into a hot bath. Can you call me back in an hour?"

"Sure. I'll call around noon."

"What? You mean it's eleven already?"

"Afraid so," Angela said. "Call you in an hour, friend."

Bonnie broke the connection, and headed back to her bath. After a half-hour's soak in the hot water, a brisk toweling, another cup of coffee, some make-up, and a brush through her hair, she felt almost civilized. While she rummaged in her refrigerator for something lunchable, the phone rang.

"It's me again, right on the dot."

"I'm feeling a little better, but I'm still not up to snuff." Forcing her mind to function, Bonnie recounted the events of the previous evening. When she got to her description of events leading to her kissing Buzz, Angela emitted a whistle and a "How about *that!*"

"So Buzz turned out to be a good guy after all, huh?"

"Too early to tell," Bonnie said. "But he was much more gentlemanly than that Skeeg guy. I wish you could have seen how carefully he re-attached the strap of my dress. He actually tried to do it without touching me." Remembering the scene, she chuckled.

"So when are you going to see him again?" Angela asked.

"Dunno. He said he'd call me when he had his new helicopter ready to fly. Said we could fly it together."

"Nice. You'll go, of course?"

"I probably shouldn't. But I think I will ... if he calls."

"Why wouldn't he?"

"Well, I *did* make something of a fool of myself last night."

"Oh, come on," Angela said. "You were recovering from a very traumatic event. Don't beat yourself up. I'd say you behaved just perfectly."

"Nice of you to say. He's polite and all ... and protective ... but he just doesn't seem interested in me as a woman."

"Why do you say that?"

"I just told you: he's polite, and attentive, but that's all. I don't think he likes me very much."

"Wait a minute. Didn't you just say he's invited you to help him fly his thingie?"

"Oh, that's right. I did."

"I'll tell you this, if I had a neighbor who came on as strongly as you did when you threatened to do him in, I'd be a little girl-shy, too."

"Okay, I get the point," Bonnie said.

"So what happens next?"

"Now I've got to think about facing Skeeg tomorrow. I'm a little nervous about that."

"If you need some advice, I'd suggest behaving as though nothing happened. That ought to reassure him."

"Maybe, maybe not. But I'll give it a try. It's going to be a busy day, what with all the preparations we need to make for the Tuesday meeting with the corporate brass. I doubt I'll see much of Skeeg. I hope not, anyway. I'm really anxious for the presentation to go well."

"How could it not?" Angela said. "You're producing whiz-bang results that oughta knock their socks off."

"I hope so." Bonnie pictured the upcoming meeting in her mind's eye. "I hope so. Uh, Angela?"

"Yes?"

"Please don't tell your husband about our conversation."

"Okay, but it's against my better judgment. I still think you should bring in the police, but I promise not to say a word—for now."

Chapter Ten

Bonnie and her two senior associates, Felina Zhang and Amalina Caruso, consumed all of Monday morning preparing visuals for Tuesday's meeting. During the afternoon, they rehearsed the presentation, sequencing the visuals for projection through her laptop computer.

"I think you could make the presentation in your sleep," Felina said. "Your last run-through was perfect. What do you think, Amalina?"

"Right on. Let's quit before she gets stale."

"Thanks, guys. I really appreciate your help. Let's pack it in and get a good night's sleep. Never know what sort of last-minute crises we'll face."

*   *   *

Tuesday dawned on another sunny day. Driving toward the Marsden plant in the outlying town of Chandler, Bonnie noted the usual smog cloud seemed lighter than usual, a good omen easing the forty-minute drive. Yeah, she thought, forty minutes ... assuming no multi-car pile-up on the free-way. She passed the time planning her day, but her mind kept wandering back to Buzz. What a re-markable man! When he's not wearing his "grung-ies," he looks like a hunk. His bulging muscles suggested his strange exercise regimen worked very well indeed. She smiled, thinking she'd like to watch him exercise on the "computer bike" that worked only while he pedaled. Mostly, though, she thought about his acts of kindness, from the time he found her shaking and sobbing on her doorstep, until he returned her to her home later that evening.

Once settled into the tiny Marsden office she'd been assigned, she answered e-mail and completed other communication chores. Deciding one more presentation run-through wouldn't hurt, she began booting her laptop just as Skeeg strode into her of-fice.

"I've decided *I'm* going to make the presenta-tion this afternoon." His manner was formal, his voice stony.

"But there's no time for you to learn it," Bon-nie protested.

"There's plenty of time. You forget, I'm expe-rienced at making presentations. Just give me the script and walk me through the visuals," he com-manded.

"What script?"

"The script for the presentation."

"There isn't any."

"What? How do you know you won't leave something out or get the numbers wrong?" he asked, sarcasm dripping from every word.

"I have a page of notes."

"Okay, give me a copy and walk me through the visuals."

"Well, all right, if you think that's best ... but I think you're making a mistake."

"Look. It's *my* department, so *I'll* decide what to do. I'll make the presentation. You'll run the projector. This project is important, you know."

"I know very well. But then, you're the client," Bonnie said, struggling to remain calm. "Why don't I just go through the presentation as I was planning to do it, and you ask questions as I go?"

"Okay," Skeeg said.

Bonnie proceeded through the talk, stopping along the way to make sure Skeeg knew which visual she was referring to, and to make sure he followed her notes as she talked.

Skeeg asked few questions, obviously thinking the presentation straightforward enough, and that his memory would be jogged by the visuals themselves.

"Okay," she said, "now it's your turn."

"No need. I think I've got it."

"You sure? What if someone asks you to go back to a previous visual?"

"No problem. I'll point to you and you'll get

the right visual projected pronto. Right?"

"Okay. Think you'll be able to handle the questions?"

"Don't patronize me," he retorted sharply. He waited impatiently until Bonnie handed him a copy of her notes, then turned and strode toward his office.

*   *   *

Bonnie arrived at the Boardroom early, planning to re-familiarize herself with the environment. A large, oval-shaped board table, surrounded by thirty comfortable swivel chairs, dominated the room. A crystal glass, already filled with water and ice, stood ready on a maroon doily at each place. Nestled beside each water glass was a pad of paper and ball-point pen. The rosewood sideboard along the wall opposite the screen served as a staging area for coffee and snacks.

A small panel controlling the projector and the room lighting had been attached to the underside of the table on a track that allowed it to be slid toward the operator when needed. For this presentation, Bonnie would sit here to control the visuals; Skeeg would stand next to the large screen.

With practiced hands, Bonnie plugged her computer into the control panel. This was her second appearance in this room, and she remembered the feeling of satisfaction when she had pressed the button raising the huge painting covering the screen mounted at one end of the room. She pressed it now and watched the painting silently disappear into the ceiling. Finally, after toggling the ceiling-mounted projector to the 'On' position, she checked its focus and slowly projected the entire slide sequence, again verifying the absence of spelling and graphics errors, and checking that the projected sequence matched her notes.

She walked around the table, positioning a copy of her report at each place. There! Everything in place and all equipment working. As her final act, she projected the Marsden logo slide that would be on-screen when the attendees arrived.

The participants drifted into the room, exchanging greetings and nodding to recognize Bonnie's presence. This high-level meeting included the CEO, the vice presidents, and division managers most directly responsible for achieving the corporation's success.

Skeeg strode into the room two minutes before the hour and headed directly toward Bonnie. "That's where *I* sit," he grunted.

"I thought you wanted me to run the projector for you," she said.

Skeeg, expecting Bonnie to move, acted as if taken aback by this frustration of his plans. "Oh ... right. Everything ready?"

She pointed to the logo projected on the screen. "All set."

Everyone having arrived by the appointed hour, John Starling, CEO, called the meeting to order.

"The only item on the agenda today," he began, "is to hear Ms. Pentera's interim report on the Sales project. As you know, that project has, as its goal, the complete revision and updating of our sales training program in anticipation of our new product lines. I'm sure I don't need to emphasize the importance of this project. So let's get started." Nodding in her direction, he said, "Ms. Pentera."

Before Bonnie could respond, Skeeg, standing next to the projection screen, spoke up. "Uh ... I decided that this project was so important, I would make the presentation myself. Bonnie will operate the visuals."

Exchanging quick glances around the table, the attendees murmured their puzzlement.

Skeeg referred to his copy of Bonnie's notes, and began the presentation. His audience listened intently, Skeeg mistakenly attributing the rapt attention to his eloquence. He warmed to his subject, becoming more expansive as he spoke.

"Yes," he said, "our early results are impressive. In all five tryout locations the results have been positive, with three-month sales figures up an average of forty percent over last year."

Whispers of incredulity rattled around the room as participants looked at one another in disbelief.

"There's more," Skeeg continued. "During those three months our attrition rate for graduates of the new course has been zero. In other words, not a single graduate has left the company. The cost saving is shown on the next slide."

Bonnie punched up the slide, amazing the participants with the size of the saving. That number, added to the number achieved by the increased sales, appeared nothing short of spectacular.

Skeeg, pleased at the admiration being expressed by those present, continued to assert his spurious ownership of the project. "Please keep in mind that what we're reporting here today are interim results. Once we've incorporated the changes suggested by the next Beta tests, the results should be even more spectacular. I believe we have created a winning product here, ladies and gentlemen."

By the time Skeeg ended the presentation, he had implied he had single-handedly masterminded the project and its results. That illusion evaporated as soon as the questions began.

John Starling, the CEO, asked, "Skeeg, aren't those results a little too good to be true?"

"Uh … I don't think so. It's all in the report you have in front of you."

"Can you add anything to that, Ms. Pentera?" asked the CEO, turning in her direction.

"Yes, sir," she began. "In truth, these results

aren't nearly as strong as those experienced by some other companies applying this technology to their own programs."

"Indeed?" the CEO said.

"Yes, sir." Bonnie described additional examples yielding stronger results.

"That's truly amazing," said Juan Cardoza, Vice President for Finance. "I had no idea we were so far behind the times with our training methodology. Turning to Skeeg, he asked, "And just what is it that makes this big improvement happen?"

Bonnie knew Skeeg had absolutely no idea what made the course work. She saw by the expression on his face that he knew he was in over his head. *Well, he deserved it,* she thought. *The bastard should have taken the trouble to learn what was going on under his nose before starting to take credit.*

Skeeg realized his moment in the sun was over. He had no answer to offer. Inwardly seething, he blamed Bonnie for this state of affairs. *She should have briefed me on the questions likely to be asked,* he thought. *But no, all she did was walk me through the presentation. She probably planned all along to leave me twisting in the wind.* His hunger for revenge intensified. "If you don't mind, I'd like Bonnie to handle that one," he said, reluctantly relinquishing the limelight.

Everyone in the room saw through his feeble

attempt to cover his ignorance.

"All right." Bonnie deliberately refrained from looking in Skeeg's direction as she spoke. She knew the implications of her being asked to take over. Expertly explaining the mechanisms that guaranteed the program's effectiveness, she concluded, "Remember, to provide motivation *without* the skills needed to actualize that motivation is like greasing the bathroom doorknob after serving Ex-Lax for dinner." The unexpected analogy resulted in an explosion of laughter.

A woman Bonnie hadn't seen before said with a laugh, "I think we *all* see your point!"

"I have just one more question for now," the CEO said, not bothering to look in Skeeg's direction. "Are you confident the program will work in the other countries—especially Asian countries?"

"Yes, sir," Bonnie responded. "As you know, cultures consist mainly of learned habits, customs, and costumes, but everyone in the world—regardless of their culture—responds to the same laws of behavior." Bonnie expanded on her answer for a full five minutes, after which the questioning continued for another half hour. Bonnie was gratified by the depth of the questions asked.

When the questioning tailed off, the CEO brought the meeting to an end. "Thank you, Ms. Pentera, for your informative comments." Turning his attention to the others, he added, "I'm sure we all agree we've the right contractor for the job."

To Bonnie's gratified surprise, an enthusiastic burst of applause followed, expressing the group's confidence in her.

On their way toward the door, several attendees took the time to shake Bonnie's hand, ask more questions, or offer a comment.

During the entire questioning period, Skeeg had remained standing beside the projection screen, completely ignored and completely frustrated. He thought back to the days of his tortured youth on the streets of New York. When the neighborhood kids discovered his father owned a junk-filled pushcart, they began calling him "Junkie." Skeeg had hated it. Already embarrassed by what his father did for a living, being jeered as "Junkie" always enraged him to a blind fury, and he always attacked the name-caller. Seldom the biggest kid in any group of tormentors, he often lost the scrap, which meant even more humiliation. Finally realizing he couldn't win that way, he learned to hide his rage as he dreamed of getting even.

Skeeg had discovered the solution to his problem one day while watching a movie wherein the villain responded to slights and insults with a smile, then later wreaked revenge when his victim least expected it. From then on, Skeeg tried responding to insults with a smile rather than a fist, while fantasizing about the revenge that would later even the score. It didn't take long to discover how many acts of revenge were readily available.

A stolen, or jammed, lock on a school locker; grease, or a dead rat in the pocket of a jacket; cut or bent bicycle spokes; a stolen bicycle seat. A zipper disabled with a pair of pliers offered delicious satisfaction while watching the frustration of a victim unsuccessfully struggling to zip up his pants. Oh, there were many ways to get even, so "getting even" became a way of life.

Skeeg's reverie ended abruptly when he realized the meeting was over and participants began moving toward the door. With a plan already half-formed, he hurried to be one of the first to exit.

After everyone had left, Bonnie packed up her equipment and materials, picked up the few reports left lying on the table, and returned to her office. Now late afternoon, she dictated a "Memo for Record" summarizing her recollections of the meeting, and prepared to leave for the day.

As she picked up her purse and briefcase, Skeeg stormed into the office.

"You deliberately sabotaged me, didn't you?" he thundered.

Bonnie immediately put her things down again; she wanted both hands free should she need them. "I did no such thing," she replied, voice icy.

"You set me up so I'd look like a fool," he continued.

"You're mistaken. You sabotaged yourself."

"What do you mean by *that?*" Skeeg snarled.

"I asked you to rehearse the presentation, and

you said you didn't need to—"

"And I was *right*. You saw how well I did it—"

"Yes. And when I asked if you would know how to answer the questions, you said I shouldn't patronize you. You have nobody to blame but yourself." Bonnie kept her voice level and as free of emotional overtone as she could manage.

But a calm recital of the facts was no way to soothe a Skeeg looking for a fight. His clenched fists made clear to Bonnie how he longed to do her physical harm.

Sensing he was on the edge of losing control, Bonnie tried to divert his attention from the cause of his fury.

"Did you notice how intently they listened to your presentation?" she asked.

"Of *course*, I noticed. I was doing a good job ... until you decided to take over."

Realizing that any response to *that* accusation would serve only to inflame him further, she tried another diversion. "Did you notice how impressed they were with the results you described?"

"Of *course*, I noticed."

"And did you notice how important the success of this project is to the company?"

"Of *course* I did."

"Then I'd better go home and get a good night's rest. There's a lot of work to be done before the next tryout."

"Don't think you can get away with treating

me like this." Skeeg turned on his heel and strode from her office, slamming the door behind him.

Bonnie stared at the just-slammed door while reviewing the events of the past two hours. *What is the problem with that man? Was that a threat?* she wondered. If so, it was time to alert other members of the Marsden organization. But what could she say—and to whom—that wouldn't jeopardize the project? Then she remembered the business card handed to her at the Ball by Mr. Cardoza. She also remembered his insistence that she call him personally should the need arise. *It's time for that call.* Reaching for her purse, she dug through the contents until the card was in her hand.

"Hello," the female voice said when she punched the number into her personal cell.

"Mrs. Cardoza? This is Bonnie Pentera. May I speak with Mr. Cardoza about the management meeting he just attended?"

A pause, followed by a click. "Good afternoon, Bonnie. I just got home and was hoping you would call."

"You were?"

"Yes, and I believe I know exactly what prompted you to do so. Ah ... we're not on a secure line, so let me just say that management is aware of the situation and I can assure you it will be dealt with within the next few days. Can you function until then?"

"I think so. Thank you for understanding."

"And thank *you* for bringing this matter to my personal attention. Please be sure to call again if anything further develops."

Chapter Eleven

Bonnie dropped her purse, briefcase, and bag of groceries onto the kitchen table, then wearily sat and kicked off her shoes.

The phone rang.

"Hi, it's me, Buzz ... from next door."

Bonnie welcomed the sound of his warm and pleasant voice. *Funny I didn't notice that before.* She thought it a nice contrast to Skeeg's belligerent snarl.

"Am I calling at a bad time?" he asked.

"Not at all. I just got home and was about to put away a few groceries."

"I think I've *got* it!" It didn't take a rocket scientist to detect the excitement in his voice.

"Got what?"

"The silent helicopter," he said. "I've finished the prototype and I'm ready for a test flight."

"Wonderful," Bonnie said, genuinely pleased at his news.

"Wanna come? Remember? I promised I'd call when I was ready."

"Uhh, when did you have in mind?" Still embarrassed by her tipsy behavior the night of Skeeg's rape attempt, she hesitated.

"Tonight, before the sun goes down," he said. "Sooner the better."

Bonnie ticked off her had-to-do's—put groceries away, freshen up, grab a quick bite.

"Uhh, if we can go sooner," Buzz put in, "I'll buy you dinner after it gets dark. How soon can I pick you up?"

"All right. How about twenty minutes?" An outing with Buzz might be just the thing to purge the Skeeg-taste from her mouth.

"Done. Don't dress up. Jeans will be fine. It's a very informal environment. And dusty."

"Where will we be going?"

"There's an RC Airfield on Cave Creek Road—"

"A *what* airfield?" Bonnie was new to the jargon of the hobby.

"Oh, sorry. RC stands for remote-controlled. It's a little airfield reserved for exclusive use by people who fly model airplanes."

"Okay, I'll be ready."

Twenty minutes later, Buzz drove into Bonnie's driveway in his red Ford pickup, a black helicopter tied to the truck bed. The rotor blades had been removed and carefully tied down beside the fuselage.

Bonnie heard the truck approaching, and opened her door before Buzz leaped from the cab.

When she glanced toward the end of the cul-de-sac, she noticed an unfamiliar car parked on the other side of the street. But by the time she'd locked her door and turned around, it was gone. She didn't give it another thought.

The drive to the RC Airfield went quickly. In that short time Buzz told Bonnie how he'd managed to silence the machine. She listened raptly.

"It's all in the details," he said. "The aluminum muffler needed to be filled with steel wool ... actually, I got a longer muffler, and then added a plastic extension."

He described other improvements, and told her about his experiments with different types and rotor blade and the importance of pitch. Though she didn't understand the technical details, she found them fascinating and grew eager to see the machine fly.

After a few minutes of driving south on Cave Creek Road, Buzz turned off into the dusty desert. As they approached their destination, Bonnie saw what looked like a very long carport with several round tables placed along its length. Remote-controlled airplanes in various stages of undress rested on four of the tables, their owner-pilots apparently making final adjustments before takeoff.

Buzz drove to the far end of the carport and parked. Then together, he and Bonnie carried the helicopter, blades, toolbox, and other gear to a concrete pad beyond the covered shed. "This pad,"

Buzz told her, "is reserved for helicopter flights; one does not, after all, fly 'copters from spaces with roofs over them."

A few minutes later, the rotors were secured in place and final flight adjustments were completed.

"Soon as I turn on the camera and digital recorder, we'll crank 'er up." He picked up his control box and flicked the appropriate switches. The box, seven inches square and two inches deep, sprouted a two-foot whip antenna from one end. "This box contains all the controls I need to fly the heli," Buzz explained. "Look. It's even got a two-inch TV screen so we can see what the camera sees."

He started the motor and the rotor blades began to turn. "Let's back off a little to a safer distance," he warned, then advanced the throttle to warm the engine.

"Is that *it?*" Bonnie asked. "Is that as loud as it gets?"

"Almost. Pretty neat, huh?"

"Unbelievable!" Bonnie lifted eyebrows at how little noise she was hearing, especially compared to the piercing whine of the model airplanes already buzzing overhead.

"Here we go." Buzz further advanced the throttle and the helicopter lifted from the ground.

"I can hardly hear it," Bonnie said, excited by the unexpected absence of the irritating whine she knew so well.

"With all the false starts and failures I've experienced, it's about time."

After hovering the craft to test its response to the controls, Buzz shot the machine almost straight up into the air.

The next few minutes were among the most intriguing Bonnie had ever experienced. Buzz put the machine through a series of maneuvers—climbs, dives, direction changes, horizontal speed runs, and more. At one point, he had the machine face in their direction while hovering a short distance away.

"Okay," Buzz said. "Go ahead and wave at yourself."

She let out a shriek of delight, as she did indeed see herself on the small control-panel screen.

"When we get home, we'll be able to play the video and see what we look like on a decent-sized screen."

"Do you have a name for this machine?" Bonnie asked, mischievously.

"Not yet. Why don't you name it?"

"Really? Okay. Umm ... how about 'Blackie'?"

"Perfect. 'Blackie' it is."

Engrossed in Blackie's antics, they didn't notice that the other hobbyists in the park had stopped what they were doing to watch this new phenomenon—a nearly-silent radio-controlled aircraft. When, at last, Buzz settled Blackie onto the landing pad, the crowd of hobbyists applauded, then gathered around to talk shop.

"I promised to buy you dinner," Buzz said, after the admirers drifted off, "but we'll have to take Blackie home first. Can't leave him in a parking lot in an exposed truck bed. Okay to drop him off before heading for a restaurant?"

"Of course."

By the time they arrived at her driveway, Bonnie had had second thoughts. "Look," she said, "it's already eight o'clock. By the time I get this desert grunge scraped off, it'll be almost nine. What say we postpone the dinner to another time?"

Buzz's face lengthened. "Well, you're probably right. By the time I get Blackie here rubbed down and put away—"

"Rubbed down?"

"Yeah. After flying the bird, I like to get the dust off and blow a little compressed air into the engine. It'll keep 'im frisky for next time."

"You're weird, you know that?" She accompanied the comment by a smile.

Buzz laughed. "I suppose all us hobby enthusiasts are a little weird. Goes with the territory." He strolled around the truck and opened the door on Bonnie's side. "If you will dismount this trusty steed, I will reluctantly walk you home."

Bonnie dismounted and curtsied. "Thank you, kind sir."

They walked to her front door. "Thanks for

coming along," he said. "It was fun having an appreciative audience."

As Bonnie watched him walk toward home, she remained puzzled—she wasn't used to men who treated her like a sister. Was there something wrong with her, she wondered? Or was he just not interested in women? No, that can't be it, she mused, wishing she had a way to peek into his head.

After a shower, Bonnie's next act was to see to Fang's needs. "How about some fresh goodies for my darling Fang," she cooed. As Fang nibbled his dinner, Bonnie related the day's events. Fang, however, seemed considerably more interested in the food.

That night, lying in bed staring at the ceiling, Bonnie's mind raced from one unsettling image to another. The presentation, the importance of the project, Skeeg's rage, and threat, the wonderful late afternoon at the RC Airfield, Buzz's seeming lack of interest in her as a woman. *What am I missing?* she wondered. During those disquieting thoughts, she drifted off to sleep.

Chapter Twelve

Buzz could hardly wait to share the news of the test with his buddy, David Chin. David and he had served together during Desert Storm days, sharing clandestine adventures in the world of intelligence. Buzz had served as a field agent responsible for collecting intelligence on the ground. David, a computer whiz, had worked to destabilize enemy computers, military operations and communications. Those had been heady days, full of dare and danger, and the two had been close friends ever since. Now, they cooperated on a variety of classified projects for the Pentagon and clandestine government organizations.

"David? Encryption."

"Got it." They simultaneously switched on their videophone encryption circuitry.

"David, I tested the new version this afternoon."

"How'd it go?"

"Pretty well. It's almost totally silent. Silent enough to amaze the hell out of the other guys at the field."

"That's good news, old buddy. How silent is it?"

"Well, I haven't put a VU meter on it yet, but I'd guess we've eliminated about 90 percent of the noise."

"Man, that's terrific!"

Buzz explained the changes he'd made since their last test and conversation. "It impressed the other hobbyists, but we've still got a way to go to meet the contract specs."

"If you'll give me the exact dimensions of the new components," David said, "along with the materials you used, I'll run a wind-tunnel simulation. Maybe I can find some clues for quieting it even more."

"Okay. Between the two of us we'll make this thing as silent as the lambs."

"We'll also make our sponsors sit up and take notice. Any idea yet how big a payload it'll carry, aside from the camera rig?"

"Not yet. But I'm convinced it'll be enough to carry several types of surveillance devices—maybe even a small weapon or two. Our sponsors are gonna be really happy."

"That's great!"

"I also impressed the hell out of Bonnie—"

"Who?"

"Bonnie, my next door neighbor."

"The one who's gonna kill you?"

"Yeah. But she says she's not mad at me any more, but I'm not so sure."

"What changed her?"

"She saw my house."

"Explain."

"When she saw my workshop basement, she decided I was a slob. Then, when she saw how neatly I keep the main house, she changed her mind. At least, that's what she says."

"Women!"

"Yeah. Go figure. I'm sure glad I'm single ... but she is kinda nice to be around."

"Been known to happen, old buddy."

"Not to me, it hasn't."

"Enjoy."

"Yeah. It's just that I don't understand how these woman things work any more and it makes me a little uncomfortable."

"How so?"

"I'm afraid if I try to kiss her she'll drop me with one of her karate chops, and I don't want to do anything to scare her off. Guess I just don't know the rules of the game anymore."

David laughed. "Man, you ain't been keeping up with the times. Next time we get together I'll be glad to explain it all to you."

"What the hell do *you* know about it? You're *married*."

"Oh, pardon me, but what's that got to do with it?"

"You can get lovin' any time you want."

"Ha," David snorted. "Shows how little you know about married life. Look. How soon can you get me those specs? I can run the simulations tomorrow if I have 'em by then."

"I'll fax 'em first thing in the morning."

Chapter Thirteen

Without turning toward Skeeg, Court Nesbitt said, "Have a seat. I'll be with you in a minute."

Skeeg did as he was told and sat at the little table in the corner of Nesbitt's office. It wasn't lost on Skeeg that Nesbitt spoke to his stand-up desk rather than to him. A bad sign, and not a good way to start the week.

Skeeg felt sure he knew what this was all about. *I'm about to have my head handed to me on a platter. And it wasn't my fault.* Without expression, he fumed at the injustice of it all. *After the way that Bonnie broad made an ass out of me at the meeting, I'll bet everybody is still laughing at me. The nerve of that bitch! I did a great presentation, and she managed to steal the attention while leaving me standing there looking like a lump. Well, not for long. It's time to get even, and I know exactly how to do it!* The thought warmed him.

"I suppose you know what I want to talk to you about," Nesbitt said, breaking into Skeeg's fantasy.

"No, sir, I don't." Wouldn't hurt to pretend innocence, Skeeg decided.

"I thought it would be obvious. All right then,
let me lay it out. I'm sure you remember our last
meeting here."

Skeeg nodded.

"During that meeting I strongly recommended
you learn what's going on in your department, and
especially that you learn about Ms. Pentera's project. You *do* remember that, don't you?" Nesbitt
opened a folder and reviewed the notes he'd made
following the meeting in question.

"Yes, sir, I remember."

"And you didn't do anything about it, did
you?"

"I certainly did! I read all of Bonnie's reports,
and I went over the presentation with her and—"

"That's hardly the same as taking steps to
learn the details of the project and assisting Ms.
Pentera with derivation of the sales course content."

"I did what I had time to do. Besides, I
thought I did a good job on that presentation.
Everybody paid attention."

"You did, and they did. But they weren't pay-
ing attention because the great Bartley Skeeg was
speaking. They paid attention because the success
of that project is critical to the continued success
of this company." Nesbitt looked Skeeg in the eyes
to let his comment sink in. "*After* your presenta-

tion, however, you couldn't answer a single question—"

"It was that Pentera woman," Skeeg interrupted. "She butted in and took over from me."

"I beg to differ. I've had a full report of what happened. The truth is you asked her to answer the questions because you hadn't a clue about how to respond. You just stood there staring and looking like an idiot."

Skeeg's body tensed, his face flushing. Under the table he clenched his fists; its glass top, however, failed to hide this reaction from Nesbitt.

"Now listen carefully, Bart. You were assigned to Training because you didn't yet have the management skills to qualify you for the Sales Manager's job, *and* because we thought that with your extensive sales experience you could contribute to the success of the Pentera project."

Skeeg was about to protest, but Nesbitt raised his hand, and continued. "You were given this job because the Training Department is one place in the company you can learn something about how all components of this organization work together. But you apparently chose not to dig in and learn the job, and chose not to provide Ms. Pentera the assistance she requires for her project. Now ... I've been instructed to tell you this is your last warning. Either you—"

"*What?* They're *firing* me? After all I've done for this company, they're kicking me out? Well, if that isn't the—"

"Bart," Nesbitt barked, "you're not listening to me. I didn't say you were fired, I said the company is offering you one last chance to step up and do the job assigned to you. So I'd advise you not to say anything you'll regret. If I were you, I'd be very careful before making accusations of ingratitude."

"This job wasn't my idea, you know."

"Yes, I know. It was the idea of a generous management trying to provide you a way to move up in the company. But now that the Pentera project has become even more important than we anticipated, your unwillingness to pitch in has become more than merely troublesome."

"I suppose they're gonna put that Pentera woman in my job," said Skeeg, his words clothed in heavy sarcasm.

"I wish we could. But she's a contractor, and company policy wouldn't allow us to offer her the position."

"I bet she'll find a way."

"You can do yourself a lot of good if you take that chip off your shoulder. Think about what I've just told you." Nesbitt rose and returned to his desk, leaving Skeeg to stare at the glass table.

*   *   *

Two afternoons later, Bonnie found herself

mired in frustration.

"Felina," she called, "do you have the 'Sales Closings' folder? I can't find it *anywhere*." She continued looking under the piles of papers and folders on her desk, filing cabinets, and even the floor.

"No, I haven't seen it." Felina, her project associate, began looking through the papers on her own desk. "I don't think Amalina has it, either, but I'll ask her."

"Damn! I just hate it when I can't find what I'm looking for. This is the third missing folder in the last two days. I feel as though I'm losing my mind, or something."

"Do you suppose Skeeg came in and took it?" Felina asked.

"Him? That was my first thought, too. But he hasn't shown any interest in what's going on in this department since he was assigned to it. What would he have to gain? I think he's too smart to do something so childish."

"Hey," Felina said, "Speaking of Skeeg, have you noticed how sweet he's been the last couple of days? All milk and honey. Wonder what's gotten into him?"

"Dunno. But the grapevine is buzzing."

"What's the gossip?"

"Rumor is that after his performance at the meeting last week, he's being tossed out on his ear."

"About time."

"Look," Bonnie warned. "Don't spread that around. It's just a rumor."

"Don't worry. It's safe with me."

A half hour later, Skeeg breezed into Bonnie's office with what looked like a smile pasted on his face.

"Good afternoon, ladies. How are things coming along?"

"Good afternoon," chimed Bonnie, Amalina, and Felina almost in unison. "Things are going just fine," Bonnie added. "We'll be ready for the next Beta test in a week or two."

"Good. Anything I can do to help move things along? I'll be available if you need me for anything."

Bonnie and Amalina looked at one another as though Skeeg had just landed from another planet. Showing interest in their work? Offering to help? What could he be snorting?

"Well," Bonnie said, "you could talk with José Barraloza in the Mexico City Division office and tell him we won't be able to use his territory for a Beta site unless he gets his paperwork back to us within the next day or two."

"José who?"

"Barraloza, Central America Sales VP. We haven't heard a word from him since the company selected his territory for the next round."

"Don't know him. Okay, give me his name and

address, and a description of what he's supposed to send, and I'll be glad to e-mail him tomorrow."

"Today would be better. We're running short of time. By the way, have you seen the 'Sales Closings' folder? We can't find it anywhere and it's driving us nuts."

"Nope, haven't seen it. You should be able to keep track of your work stuff better than that."

When Skeeg left, the three women shook their heads in disbelief. "Dear God," Amalina said, "I sure hope that rumor is true."

Skeeg walked toward his office with a satisfied grin on his face. *Now for Plan B.*

Chapter Fourteen

The information from Barraloza still had not arrived by noon the following day. Bonnie brooded at her desk, tapping her teeth with her pen. Did Skeeg, or did he not, follow through as promised? She began to doubt it. Wincing at the implications, she decided to wait one more day before calling to inform Mr. Barraloza she would have to move the tryout to another territory.

Amalina burst into her office and thrust a manila folder under Bonnie's nose. "Look at this."

"What is it?"

"The 'Sales Closings' folder you couldn't find the other day."

"Wait a minute. I didn't give you that folder. Where did you find it?"

"On the floor behind my filing cabinet."

"On the *floor? Behind* your filing cabinet? How in the world did it get there?" Butterflies fluttered in Bonnie's stomach. The same warning jitters she had felt on noticing the folder's absence now returned in full. Feeling comfortable only when in full control of her life, she found this more than merely disconcerting; it gnawed at her very foundations.

"I've no idea," Amalina replied. "*I* certainly didn't put it there. Could the office cleaners have done it?"

"They could, I suppose, but I can't imagine why. Let's talk to Felina. Maybe she knows something."

The two of them trooped down the hall to the small conference room where Felina sat studiously transferring data from computer printouts to charts. Bonnie recounted the case of the missing folder and it's rediscovery.

"Sorry, guys. I haven't a clue."

"Until we solve the mystery of the migrating folders, we've got to be careful about how we handle them. We don't want a repeat of this incident. Let's all try to make sure we lock everything up before we leave the building."

*   *   *

On her way home that afternoon, Bonnie stopped at the supermarket to re-stock her dwindling supply of food, both for herself and Fang. Like the good trouper her father taught her to be, she always kept her larder generously supplied. Not only did that help avoid unexpected shortages, buying in quantity also helped her food budget.

She was a careful shopper.

When she reached the checkout counter with her fully-loaded cart, Bonnie watched closely, as usual, as the clerk rang up the groceries, sliding each tallied item to her left.

"Wait a minute!" Bonnie said, pointing to the bottle of cheap wine about to be rung up by the clerk. "That's not mine."

The clerk frowned as if annoyed by the break in her rhythm. "I jest took it from the things you piled on the counter, honey."

"I don't care. It's not mine."

The clerk stopped her processing and stared. Obviously casting Bonnie as one of those mentally deficient people recently forced back on the streets by the local asylum, she stood rooted in place, uncertain of her next move.

Bonnie resented the stare. "Look. Somebody must have put that into my basket by mistake. You'll probably ring up a shopper who's missing a bottle of wine."

"Yeah. Could be." With an exasperated flourish, the clerk set the bottle aside and continued recording the remaining items.

Bonnie tried not to show it, but the incident was unsettling. It was a minor thing, but with all that had been happening, it rattled her. Never before had anything like this happened—ever. *Am I losing my sanity? Come on, I'm a careful shopper; I never put anything into my cart until I scrutinize the label.*   She was reminded of an elderly shopper she'd once seen who couldn't remember placing any of the items into her basket. *Am I going to get that senile, too?* She shook her head to clear the image from her mind. *All right,* she told herself, *just get a grip!*

Her resolve, however, was short-lived.

At home, when putting the items into their assigned places, her hand suddenly stopped in mid-air.

What the devil? In her hand she held three cans of cat food. *Cat food? Damn. I distinctly remember putting three cans of tuna fish into my basket. How can they have been replaced by cat food? Have I grown so careless that I didn't notice the difference? No. Impossible! Besides, pet foods and tuna fish are stored on different aisles. There's no way I could have made such a foolish mistake.*

Bonnie leaned against the counter and stared at the cat food in her hands, mentally retracing her steps through the store. No! There was no way she could have made such a gross error unless ... unless she was losing her mind.

*   *   *

Sleep was slow in coming that night. When, at long last, she had drifted into an uneasy sleep, the phone rang, as if awaiting that exact moment. It rang several times before a groggy Bonnie awakened enough to grope for the instrument.

"Hullo?" She heard nothing but heavy breathing.

"Look, is this some kind of sick joke or something?"

The heavy breathing continued.

"Look, you creep! You call here again and I'll blow out your eardrums!" Angrily, she slammed down the phone.

Returning to sleep took even longer than before. At four in the morning, the phone rang again. Rather than answer, she turned off the phone, fuzzily hoping she'd remember to turn it on in the morning.

When the morning sun began peeking into her windows, Bonnie rose early and, after turning her phone back on, prepared to return the cat food to the supermarket on her way to work. Tired from the interruptions of her sleep pattern, she treated herself to a long shower, then put on her favorite outfit—light blue skirt and matching jacket over a white silk blouse. There! Eyeing herself in her full-length mirror, she exclaimed, "This outfit will surely make the day go better."

At the supermarket, she explained to the first clerk whose attention she could attract, "These cans of cat food got into my basket by mistake. I'd like to exchange them for the tuna fish I remember putting in my cart."

The clerk barely spoke English, and Bonnie had to describe her problem twice more before her simple message got through. Finally, the clerk took the cat food cans, and led Bonnie to the tuna fish department. Since there was a price difference, it took time to calculate the minuscule price adjustment. That made her late for work.

Now out of sorts because of the cat food incident leading to her tardiness, she started the final site selections for the forthcoming tryout.

Partway through the task, Felina tripped hurriedly into Bonnie's office, then screeched to a halt. "You're *here,*" she exclaimed in surprise.

"Of course, I'm here."

"I've been trying to call you and I can't even get your phone to ring."

"What are you talking about?" Another seed of alarm sprouted in Bonnie's consciousness. "There's nothing wrong with my phone."

She lifted the phone from its cradle and put it to her ear. No dial tone.

"*Damn!*" she exploded. "Now the phone's dead. What next?" She banged the phone into place and leaped to her feet.

"Felina, do me a favor."

"Sure."

"Call Maintenance and ask them to come fix my phone. And tell them to hurry. I'm expecting a call from Mexico City."

An hour later, a phone specialist from Maintenance arrived and busied himself with Bonnie's phone.

"There's nuthin' wrong with the phone, ma'm, it's just—"

"What do you mean, there's nothing wrong. It's *dead!*"

"What Ah was about to say is that there ain't nothin' wrong with the phone itself. Y'all jist managed to unplug it from the phone jack on the wall." He held up the end of the phone cord for her to see.

"What? I did no such thing. When I left yesterday afternoon it was working perfectly."

"Well, it didn't unplug itself." He inserted the phone jack, checked for a dial tone, and offered the handset for Bonnie's confirmation. "It's workin' now. See?"

Bonnie listened to the dial tone for some seconds and again slammed the phone into its nest. As soon as she removed her hand, it rang. She picked it up and barked into it a hard, "Hello!"

"Good morning," Skeeg said, his tone oily. "Why haven't you been answering your phone?"

"I haven't been answering my phone because it hasn't been ringing, and it hasn't been ringing because the cord was *disconnected*." The rasp in her voice expressed her frustration.

"Why did you do that?" Skeeg said, enjoying Bonnie's distress.

"I *didn't* do it," Bonnie snapped. "I've no idea

how it happened."

"Well, whatever, it seems to be working fine now."

Bonnie decided the time had come to change the subject. "Look, Bart, did you e-mail Barraloza like you promised you would?"

"Sure did," he lied. "Haven't you heard from him?" Skeeg had to work to keep the glee from showing in his voice.

"I haven't heard a peep from him and I'm going to have to cross him off the tryout list."

"He's not going to like that."

"Tough. If he can't take the time to communicate, I have no other choice." The wisp of a thought crossed her mind. *No, it can't be Skeeg's work. Sure, he's an arrogant, self-centered pain in the ass, but he's bright and ... well ....* She let the thought slip from her consciousness.

When they ended the call, Skeeg put down his phone and banged his desk with the flat of both hands. "Hot damn!" he shouted, loudly enough for his secretary in the outer office to hear. *More fun than I've had in years. Yes,* he gloated, *this was definitely one of my better ideas. As for you, bitch, there's more to come. Lots more.* Opening his computer file labeled "Bitch," he scanned the list of evil tactics he'd drafted. "Okay. What'll I do next?"

Chapter Fifteen

On arriving home, Bonnie dragged herself into the house. Her first act was to look after Fang. "What good did it do me to wear my favorite outfit, huh?" she asked the bird.

Fang chirped.

"That's easy for *you* to say," she continued, "but it didn't help me one darn bit. I had to waste time returning the cat food, was late for work, then had to have my dead phone fixed. Barraloza *still* hasn't responded and, to top it all off, I couldn't find my stapler. *Anywhere.* It's as if every speed bump in the world was being dragged across the highway of my life. It's even worse than getting a fruitcake for Christmas, for God's sake!"

Bonnie's weariness deepened. It had been hard enough trying to sleep the night before, but the late-night calls from the heavy breather made that quest practically impossible. *Well, there's only one thing to do at a time like this—slip into a cool shower.* As soon as the idea formed, her spirits brightened. She disrobed en route to the bath-

room. Adjusting the water to the right temperature, she stepped into the oversized stall. Luxuri-
ating in the feel of the soothing liquid streaming
down her body, she sucked in several deep
breaths, trying to clear her mind of recent troubles. "Ahh, nothing like a shower to dissolve the
cobwebs."

Thoroughly refreshed, she dried herself with
the large, fluffy bath towel hanging just outside the
shower door. The phone rang.

"*Ha!*" Bonnie barked at the cordless phone
she'd placed on the bathroom sink. "Fooled 'ya,
didn't I?" She was pleased she'd remembered to
carry the instrument with her. It was so frustrat-
ing when the phone rang and she couldn't even
find it. Smugly, she grabbed it up.

"Hi. It's me—Buzz."

The sound of his voice made her feel warm all
over. "Hi-i-i," she said in her most seductive voice.

"Hope I'm not calling at a bad time."

"Not at all." Bonnie imagined Buzz standing
naked in his own bathroom. *Maybe this day will
end on an upbeat, after all.*

"I just wanted to tell you I turned your water
off."

"What are you talking about?"

"You left your outside faucet running when
you left this morning."

"I *what?* Where?"

"The one on the back of your house. The hose

nozzle had been taken off, and the water just ran into your yard. You'll probably have a pretty big bill this month."

"Look. I haven't done anything in the yard since last Sunday, and there's no *way* I could have left the water running. What's going on?" Bonnie's voice tightened, rising in pitch.

"These things happen. I just wanted to let you know I turned it off a little before noon."

"What made you notice it?" she asked.

"Blackie happened to be peeking over your wall. Accidentally. I think he misses you."

Oh, that's great! That's ... just ... great! The damned helicopter misses me. How nice. What about the lummox who's telling me this? Doesn't he miss me, too? He sends an inanimate object to flirt with me, then uses it to play John Alden? What the hell's the matter *with this guy?*

"How nice," she managed to say.

"He wasn't snooping or anything. I was just adjusting a lens and he accidentally took a quick peek."

"Terrific," Bonnie retorted, a bit more testily than she had intended. "And had I been sunning in the yard, I suppose he would have made another tape to add to your collection?"

Buzz didn't know how to respond. *What is the* matter *with this woman? I thought she liked Blackie. After all, she's the one who named him. I make a courtesy call to tell her I turned off her*

faucet she left running, and suddenly she's pissed
at me. She gonna kill the messenger?

"Are you gonna kill me again?" he asked.

Bonnie realized she was being irrational.
"Look," she said, trying to regain her composure.
"I'm sorry, okay? I've just had a couple really bad
days. I guess I'm spoiling for a fight."

"Wanna talk about it?"

"No. What I want right now is to put on my
pajamas, have a quiet meal, and do a little reading
before bed. I didn't get much sleep last night."

"Okay. Sorry about the faucet, though. I just
thought you'd be glad somebody turned it off."

"I *am* glad somebody turned it off, and I'm
sorry if I sounded ungrateful. It's just ... it's just
that I've had a couple of rough days and I need
some peace and quiet ... and I'm ticked because I
don't know how the faucet got turned on in the
first place."

"I understand. I'll hang up and leave you in
peace. But ... Bonnie? Still got the alarm button I
gave you?"

"It's in my purse."

"Keep it close. 'Night."

Bonnie slumped onto her closed toilet lid, staring at the phone in her hand. *This really is too*
much! I've heard of bad things happening in
threes, but this is ridiculous. She pondered the
running water situation, trying to fathom the
cause. She knew it wasn't something she'd done

by accident, and she hadn't had any service people at the house for more than a month. *But the nozzle was taken off? That's mean. If I ever catch those neighborhood hoodlums near this house, I'll give them more than a piece of my mind.*

With this latest unsolved mystery spinning in her head, she donned her pajamas and headed for the kitchen. She wasn't in the mood to cook, so satisfied herself with a cucumber salad and a piece of leftover chicken, followed by a left-over pear half for dessert.

It wasn't long before her thoughts again turned to Buzz. That was a strange situation as well—him thinking of her. *Sometimes, he seems genuinely concerned about my welfare; other times, he seems so aloof. No, not aloof. He just acts as though I'll break if he gets too close.* For the umpteenth time, she searched for explanations. *There must be something about me he doesn't find attractive. If it weren't so brazen, I'd just ask him.*

Sleep improved over that of the night before, but restlessness continued. Thank God she'd remembered to turn off her phone.

The following morning being Saturday, Bonnie slept in—all the way until eight am. Pulling on robe and slippers, she opened her front door and reached for the morning paper. It wasn't there. Thinking evil thoughts about the delivery boy, she looked around the immediate area and, finding nothing, expanded her search. Still nothing.

"That's it," she grumped at the empty porch. "All I need is for the bleeping *Republic* to be late delivering again." With a determined march, she trooped to the phone and banged in the number of the *Arizona Republic* circulation department. Drumming her fingers on the counter while fumbling through the endless litany of irritating voicemail menus, a darkening scowl formed on her face. At last, she was finally connected to a real, live human being.

Identifying herself, she asked, testily, "What time will the paper be delivered this morning?"

The voice checked records, then said, "I'm sorry ma'am, but the records show that you canceled your subscription as of this morning and—"

"I did no such thing!" Bonnie's agitated voice rose in pitch like a wailing siren. "I don't know what you're talking about. There must be some mistake."

"Sorry. I've checked it twice. The caller canceled your subscription three days ago, to start today."

"And just *who* canceled the subscription?" Bonnie made her voice sound as ominous as she knew how.

"Your husband."

"My what?"

"Your husband."

"Look, you ..." With difficulty, Bonnie restrained herself from calling the voice a nincompoop. "Look here," she said, starting over, "I don't *have* a husband. I don't even have a *dog*."

"I'm sorry—"

"Okay. Just re-instate my subscription. Got it? And send me a paper."

"I'll be happy to take care of your order." The voice verified the subscription information and politely ended the call.

Still fuming, Bonnie slammed down the phone. *My God,* she thought, *you don't suppose Skeeg ... oh, come on, don't go there. But still ...* Sipping her coffee as best she could with shaking hands, she called Angela. "Angela, I've got to talk to you."

"What's up? You sound upset?"

"There's something going on and I don't know what it is. What I *do* know is that it's driving me crazy—"

"Slow down, girl."

"—and I don't know what to do about it."

"Take a deep breath, okay?"

"Never mind that. Is your husband working tonight?"

"Yeah, he's got the four-to-midnight shift. Why?"

"I think I may need to talk to him. Can you meet me for a snack late this afternoon? There's a movie playing at Fashion Square that's supposed to be really funny, and funny is what I need right now."

"Uh ... sure. Cop-husband Tony's still here, if you want to talk to him."

"No, thanks. Not over the phone."

"We could talk during our workout session."

"No."

"Why not?"

"I don't *know,* Angela. All I'm sure of is that I want to sit across a little table from you and sip a milk shake when I tell you about it. Maybe we can make some sense of it together. Let's make it at four o'clock. Okay?"

"Okay, but for now, take some deep breaths. Please!"

Chapter Sixteen

It was dark by the time Bonnie drove into her garage. Though her talk with Angela had been soothing, it had solved nothing. As Bonnie described the mysterious events at great length, Angela offered rational explanations for each. Bonnie began to feel better, yet, deep down, she was convinced there *had* to be another explanation.

"I can see how the stapler could have gotten lost, and the phone might have become unplugged," Bonnie said. "But the water faucet couldn't have turned on by itself, nor could the nozzle be unscrewed without help."

"Yes, but it could have been a prank by a neighborhood kid. Or a kid who turned it on to get a drink, then forgot to turn it off."

"Yeah, I suppose. Now that we've talked it out, I'm feeling a little better," Bonnie said, "but it still seems like an awful lot of coincidences. Pranks or not, they make me feel as though I'm losing control. My God, Angela, if Buzz hadn't noticed, the water might *still* be running. And if he hadn't called, I might never have known about it until I got a monster bill from the water company."

She was still uneasy. The sheer number of unexpected frustrations was simply more than she could handle with equanimity. Sure, she was a self-assured and independent woman. But this was too much.

She turned her key in the lock of the kitchen door connecting to the garage, entered, and toggled the light switch. As soon as the light came on, she realized something was wrong. An instant later, she knew *several* somethings were wrong. Walking slowly through the kitchen, she noted the coffee maker no longer sat in its place to the left of the sink; it was now to the right. The contents of her utensil drawer had been dumped into the sink. When she pulled out the drawer to see what was left, she found the drawer had been replaced upside down.

Her anxiety rising, she hurried on to the small dining area, immediately noticing the four dining room chairs facing away from the table, with the throw rug slid under it.

Bonnie's first glimpse of the living room further raised her alarm. Her TV had been dragged to the other end of the wall, gouging her wood floor. Pictures on the walls had been interchanged.

Someone's been in my house! She recalled the feeling of violation the "Three Bears" must have felt. In a flash her mind jumped to the next logical thought—is the culprit *still* in the house, waiting for my arrival? Now near panic, she called, "Hello? Is someone here?"

No response.

Her hands began shaking as her breathing grew more rapid. This is too much! Gripped by an invisible force, she decided she couldn't handle this alone. She needed help. Remembering the panic button Buzz had given her for just such emergencies, she dug frantically in her purse.

Finding her unsteady hands unequal to the task, she ran to the kitchen table and turned her purse upside down on its surface. There it was at last! She pressed the button, hard.

Nothing! No screech! No horns! No sirens! *Nothing!*

She pressed it again, and again. Near tears at the absence of an immediate response, she jabbed at the button, over and over.

Just as she realized she should leave the house—now!—the doorbell rang. Startled at the unexpected sound, Bonnie screamed and ran to the utility closet. Grabbing the hammer she kept there, she held it over her head and tiptoed back to the door.

"It's me—Buzz," he called. "Bonnie, open the door."

"Thank God," she breathed, rushing to unlock the front door. It was thoughtless of her not to have unlocked the door as soon as she'd pressed the panic button. Now she was panicked *and* embarrassed.

She opened the door, still poised to strike an intruder. As soon as she recognized her neighbor, she lowered the hammer, and fell into his arms. Burying her face in his chest, his arms encircling her, she let go of her pent-up frustrations and sobbed.

Buzz waited until her sobs slowed to occasional hiccuping sighs before asking the question. "What's wrong, Bonnie?"

"Some ... somebody's ... been in my house. He's moved everything around. And he might still be *in* here."

At those words, Buzz gently guided Bonnie to one side of the door.

"Stay here and don't move. I'll check it out."

Buzz lifted the front of his sweatshirt and removed a semi-automatic pistol from his waistband. With a firm, decisive movement, he pulled the slide back and let it snap forward, seating a cartridge into the chamber. He held it in front of him with his right hand, and braced it with his left. Flicking a small switch on the side of the pistol caused a thin infra-red beam to shoot out, guiding his aim. Moving quickly, he checked one room after another until satisfied he had "cleared" the entire house.

Stuffing the gun into his waistband, he returned to Bonnie, who still trembled beside the front door. He wrapped his arms around her and soothingly stroked her hair, whispering reassurances. "The house is clear. There's no one here now."

"My ... my whole life ... is coming ... apart," she said between sobs. "I ... I don't ... know what's ... *happening*." She again buried her face in his chest to hide tears she couldn't stop.

"Well, *I* do," Buzz soothed, "and I can assure you it won't go on much longer."

Bonnie lifted her head from his chest and looked at his eyes. "What do you mean? You *know* what this is all about? Tell me."

"First, we lock the house and get you over to my place. Then I'll tell you what I know."

Bonnie was in no mood to object, or to assert herself. Trudging to the kitchen, she locked the door to the garage, and put the scattered items back into her purse. After checking the back door, they went out the front, where she used her key to lock both the door lock and deadbolt.

With his supporting arm around her waist, Buzz led her across the lawns to his front door. After settling her into one of his overstuffed chairs, he left the room for a moment, returning with a small snifter of brandy.

"Here. Drink this. It'll help you relax."

Bonnie looked up with grateful eyes. "You tryin' to get me sozzled again?"

Buzz laughed, deciding her attempt at humor

was a good sign. "You bet. These days, you can't expect to get anywhere with a beautiful woman unless you first get her flat-out drunk."

"That's a lie!" Even so, she swallowed a large gulp.

"That's better." When she took another sip, Buzz added, "You're beginning to fight back already, and I thank you for not clobbering me with that hammer."

Bonnie took another sip. "Think nothing of it. But I admit, I was scared enough to flatten the first unfamiliar face I saw. Now tell me what this is all about ... or do I have to beat it out of you?"

Buzz held his arms in front of him in a defensive stance. "Please, lady, don't hurt me. I'll tell, I'll tell. It's Bartley Skeeg."

Her raised eyebrows revealed her astonishment. "Skeeg? I *knew* it! Well, I did and I didn't." Her mind whirled to put the pieces together. "How do you know? He hasn't shown any interest in what I'm doing, so why would he bother to do *this*? How can it be him?"

"There's been a black BMW parked out at the end of the cul-de-sac during the evenings."

"Uh-huh. I think I saw it once. But I didn't make anything of it. So?"

"So I sent Blackie out the other night to get the license plate number."

"In the dark?"

"No problem. I attached the infra-red camera

and sent Blackie circling around so the driver
wouldn't see him. When Blackie was behind the
BMW I had him settle lower, but not low enough
to be seen in the rear-view mirror. It was a simple
matter to read the number on the plate."

"Wow! And it was Skeeg's car?"

Buzz nodded. "I had someone run the number
through the police files."

"*You* can do *that?*" Bonnie was amazed at the
unexpected powers of this seemingly gentle man.
What would he do next—leap tall buildings in a
single bound?

"Not personally. My friend, David Chin, did
it."

"I thought he lived in California."

"He does, Bonnie. But he has powerful computers, and he knows how to use them."

The situation began to look much rosier than
it had when she arrived home. She noticed her
hands shook hardly at all, and her breathing was
almost normal. "But why is Skeeg doing this?"

"Remember my telling you the night he tried
to rape you that he might escalate? That's what
he's doing."

"But why?"

"I'm certain that in his mind, you're the cause
of all his problems."

"That's not true."

"Of course not. *You* know that and *I* know
that. But in *his* warped mind, he's fixated on you.

Even with all that's happened, he probably still thinks of you as his 'girlfriend.' At the same time, he believes you've humiliated him more than once. At the dance, you embarrassed him in front of his subordinates. When he attacked you, you laid him on the ground as easily as if he were a five-year-old kid. And later on, you mentioned to me that you showed him up as incompetent during a presentation to the vice presidents."

"Well, he deserved it."

"Of course he did. But in his mind, you've committed the unforgivable sin. So he *has* to get even; he *has* to get revenge. He *has* to."

"My God, and he's the one stalking me?"

"Yes. And his type won't stop until he's destroyed the person he's decided is responsible for humiliating him and getting the better of him in a physical contest. That's why he's stalking you."

Bonnie withdrew into the cushions of the chair. This was a lot to digest. *I'm the target of a stalker? My God—just like on television—except there the stalker gets his in the end ... and I don't have a clue about what to do.*

"What am I gonna do?" she asked, her voice barely audible.

Buzz leaned toward her and took her hands in his. "You don't have to take this lying down, Bonnie, any more than you accepted his physical attack lying down."

"So?"

"So we're going to fight back."

Bonnie's voice hardened. "What do you mean—*we?*

"I'm offering to help get Skeeg off your back once and for all, Bonnie. What's wrong with that?"

"I'm sorry. It's just that, well, I'm not used to having to lean on people, and—"

"And so you're gonna kill me again for offering?"

"No, no. I didn't mean that. I … I'm still rattled. Of course I'd welcome your help. But what can we do?"

"We can beat him at his own game. First off, you can go to the police—"

"*No!* No police. I promised if he wouldn't interfere with my project, I wouldn't tell the police or anyone at the company. Besides, I don't believe the police could do anything, especially since he hasn't broken any law."

"He broke into your house and gouged your floor—"

"Can we prove that? Anyway, I still don't want the police. But still, I will *not* have him interfering with my project."

"Okay, scratch that option. On to Plan B."

Bonnie stared into her empty brandy snifter, then held it toward Buzz. "Got any fizzy water? I need to go easy on this stuff."

With an amused smile, Buzz made a round trip to the kitchen and handed her a tall glass of sparkling water, then repeated his earlier comment. "Did you hear me? We go to Plan B."

She heard the words, but the meaning wasn't entirely clear. "Yeah, Plan B."

"Yes, Plan B. And we can begin any time you're ready."

"I ... I still don't know what to do. Uh ... what's Plan B?"

"When you're ready, I'll tell you all about it. Then we'll begin. Right here. Tonight. Right now!"

Chapter Seventeen

Buzz led his guest toward the large room he referred to as his den.

Bonnie glanced around the room and decided it wasn't—a den, that is. It was an office. No, not an office, either. She decided it was more like a control center. The room was filled floor-to-ceiling and wall-to-wall with equipment, some familiar to her, some not. She recognized the office equipment. She also recognized a computer tower standing under a U-shaped desk, as well as the large twenty-eight inch computer monitor, and the split keyboard.

But scanning to the right of the computer desk, she saw equipment she didn't recognize at all.

Noting her puzzlement, Buzz said, "That thing over there is a short-wave radio, and the little box next to it is a scrambler."

"A what?"

"Scrambler. It's for encrypting phone calls and video signals, through both the computer and land-line, so conversations can't be understood by prying busybodies."

"Why would you need to do that?"

"Uhh, I'd rather not get into that right now. But I'll show you part of the answer to that in just a minute." Buzz rolled a spare office chair over next to his at the computer, and bowed. "Please to have a seat."

Bonnie sat—and stared in awe as his fingers played over the keyboard like a piano virtuoso. Within seconds, a face appeared in a window in one half of the large monitor's screen. Buzz and Bonnie's images appeared in the other half.

"Hi, Ram," said the voice.

"Encrypt." A second or two passed, during which the picture was replaced by jagged lines for three seconds, after which it settled down again.

"David Chin, meet Bonnie Pentera, my neighbor."

"Pleased to meet you," the face said, nodding.

Bonnie smiled. Chin seemed pleasant—even serene. His obvious Asian ancestry added interest, his dark eyes and hair suggesting a life of intrigue.

Buzz said, "David and I go back to Desert Storm days. This boy just might be the mightiest computer virtuoso who ever lived. Now we work together on the same sort of projects, but without the uniforms."

"What kind of projects?"

"Uhh, we can't go into that just now."

"You mean they're secret?"

"Something like that." Changing the subject, Buzz said, "Dave, we've got a hot project."

"Go."

"Bonnie is being stalked and can't go to the police. I'll fill you in on that part later."

"Target?"

"The same one you checked out the other day."

"Right." Quickly retrieved by David's flying fingers, information began appearing on the screen: Skeeg's address, driver's license number, social security number, employer, employer's address and telephone number.

"Yep, that's the guy."

"Mission?"

"Get this creep off Bonnie's back once and for all."

"Terminate?"

"No. The target's not a professional—just a sicko."

"Okay. Can I ask Bonnie some questions?"

"Of course." Turning his attention to Bonnie, Buzz said, "David needs more information before we settle on a plan. Okay?"

"Sure ... I guess." Bonnie sat stiffly beside Buzz, bewildered by this conversation between two highly-trained professionals. But professionals at what? She couldn't say. Her life experience hadn't included contact with such people—yet she found it strangely exhilarating, and burned with curiosity to know more.

David asked, "Bonnie, I need to know why Bartley Skeeg is stalking you."

"I don't know ... not for sure."

"I think you do. You're definitely among friends here, and nobody can overhear our conversation, so you can be candid. Why is he stalking you?"

"Uh, okay. I see what you mean. I think he's stuck on the idea that I'm his girlfriend. I think he got that idea because I took him to a business lunch one day and later agreed to accompany him to the company Ball. He told several people that I'm his girlfriend, and that we have a relationship. I've insisted several times it isn't true, but he doesn't listen."

"Uh huh," David said, typing and nodding at the same time. "I know the type, but there's more, isn't there?"

"Yes." Bonnie reluctantly went on to tell him about the attempted rape, about the way she thwarted Skeeg's attack, and about the times she unintentionally humiliated him in front of others.

"Got it. Bonnie, I'm going to need some information about Mr. Skeeg's habits. I'll send you some questions; Ram can print them out for you."

Questions scrolled down Buzz's screen:
- What building does he work in?
- Where is his office located, precisely?
- Anyone else work in his office?

- Secretary's name and phone number, if any?
- Where does he park his car? Exactly?
- Work hours? Usual arrival and departure times?
- Computer: name and model number?
- Is his computer networked?

"Anything else you can find out about him, without being obvious, could be helpful. If you can dig some papers out of his wastebasket, that would help, too. But don't do anything risky."

"My God," Bonnie exclaimed. "What in the world are you planning to do with all that information?"

"We won't know until we look at what we have. But the speed with which we can accomplish our mission depends on the data you collect. Okay?"

"Yeah, okay." Dazzled by what she saw as "cloak and dagger stuff," she wondered what she was getting into.

David added another caution. "Bonnie, there's just one more thing for now. If you write any of the information down, do not enter it into your computer."

"Why not? Nobody but me uses my computer, and I'm the only one who knows the passwords."

"You wanna explain, Ram?"

"Sure." Turning to Bonnie, Buzz said, "Bonnie, David can read everything—*everything*—you've got stored in your computer, and so can lots of other people."

"What? But they don't know my *passwords,*" she protested.

"Doesn't matter. A skilled hacker can slide through those like a hot knife through butter."

"Now you're scaring me." Bonnie frowned and scrunched her shoulders at the suggestion of anyone reading the files stored on her hard drive.

"That's the idea," Buzz said, nodding.

Glancing at the screen, Bonnie noticed David was nodding, too. "It's something you *should* be frightened about," Buzz continued. "Some evening when we're sitting by the fire, I'll tell you all about it."

Bonnie's antennae didn't miss the words Buzz had just spoken—"sitting by the fire." That had a nice sound to it, one that triggered a pleasant fantasy. But what did he mean? Had that been an unintentional peek at his intentions? Was he saying he actually liked her—or better yet, was attracted to her—enough to harbor thoughts about their spending quiet evenings by the fire? Her heart soared. For just a moment, she let her mind wander farther into the fantasy, and imagined herself living in this very house with Buzz, teasing him about his messy basement, and living happily ever after. The fantasy dissolved when she heard David speak.

"When do you think you'll have something for us?" he asked.

"Oh. Uh ..." Shaking off the fantasy tentacles still clinging to her mind, she said, "I believe I can have most of it by Monday afternoon. Tomorrow's Sunday, but I don't think I can get much then."

"That'll be fine," David said, smiling. "Ram and I will do a little preliminary planning until then."

"You want me to tell Buzz about anything I learn?"

"Buzz? Who's Buzz?" David Chin asked, frowning.

"Not to worry," Buzz said. "She calls *me* Buzz, and I'll fill you in on that later, too. Bye for now."

"Bye for now." They each broke their connection and vanished from the screen.

"What are you two planning to do?" Bonnie asked. Suddenly, she felt like an outsider looking in. This was *her* problem, she thought, and *her* fight. Though grateful for the masterful way Buzz took charge of the situation, and appreciative of his help, it was still *her* problem, and *her* fight. She wasn't about to be locked out of it.

Buzz swiveled in her direction and took her hands in his. "We're going to give Skeegy-boy a dose of his own medicine. Except that what's been happening to you is nothing compared to what we'll plan for him. That kind of guy doesn't respond well to anything he considers a disruption to his life."

"What do you mean?"

"You saw how he responded when you resisted his attack, and when you refused to fall into his 'relationship' fantasy. Those disturbed him so much he's started stalking you, doing nasty things."

"Yes, I see what you mean."

"You've also seen how he's been escalating. First the little things like stealing folders, then working his way up to breaking into your house and moving things around."

Bonnie shuddered. Now that she realized how easy it was for someone to break into her home and her computer, she felt apprehensive about returning to her empty house.

"Yes," Buzz said, reading her mind. "Once we get started on our own sequence, he's going to go wild. He can't help it. So I'm not going to let you stay home at night because—"

"Wait a minute. You're not going to *let* me stay in my own house?"

"Sorry. I used the wrong words. Look, Bonnie. I care about what happens to you. I ... I don't have the words for talking about things like this, but ... uh ... in just the short time we've known each other, I've become rather fond of you. And that goes for Blackie and Heli, too."

Bonnie giggled, and Buzz's face fell.

Oh, my God! He thinks I'm laughing at him. What an ass I am ... I've ruined the moment. "I'm really sorry, Buzz. I wasn't snickering at what you were saying. It's just that when you mentioned

Blackie and Heli, I suddenly remembered a ventriloquist friend of mine. His wife often jokes about how she never knows how many guys there are in bed with her."

When Buzz joined her laughter with a chuckle, Bonnie continued. "I'm truly sorry I interrupted your train of thought. Please go on."

"My lecture was almost over. It's just that, well, I like having you around, and I don't want to expose you to any harm."

"That's sweet of you. I appreciate it—a lot."

"As for not staying in your own home, I guess you should be okay there for the next few days. Things won't get really rough on Skeeg until later in the week. We'll have to see what David and I come up with."

"You're not going to hurt him, are you?"

"We'll try not to, but if the need arises, we'll do whatever we have to do to neutralize the situation. Our goal will be to give him so much to do he won't have time to pay any attention to you. What's more, we want to do it in a way that won't give him any reason to suspect you have anything to do with his life crashing around his ears. That's critical. Your safety is our number-one priority, but as I said, we'll do *whatever* it takes to neutralize the threat."

They both came to their feet, with Buzz holding Bonnie's hands. This close, he stared into her deep blue eyes, realizing how terribly upset he would be if anything happened to Bonnie.

"Bonnie, would you mind ... very much if I ... kissed you?" he asked, hesitantly.

"I think I'd like that very much." *At last!*

"You promise not to kill me if I do?"

"Not a chance," she murmured, lifting her head as she wrapped her arms around his neck. "Just don't let go."

Their lips touched, lightly at first, and then more firmly, each feeling the thrill arising from their very first kiss. Buzz breathed in her pleasant fragrance, pleased it wasn't jasmine. Nothing wrong with jasmine, he reasoned stupidly at this moment, except it had been the favorite perfume of a woman to whom he'd been engaged for an entire three weeks. She broke it off when she discovered Buzz wasn't about to give up his work and hobbies to pamper her totally unrealistic social ambitions. He, in turn, broke it off when he discovered she couldn't have children, didn't want to adopt any, and didn't want any around the house, thank you very much. It was a bitter memory coloring his contacts with women ever since. But Bonnie had always smelled alluring, so nice ... so sweet. Was it gardenia? He tossed his thoughts aside and gave himself whole-heartedly to the kiss, his body tingling.

Melting into his arms, Bonnie felt the kiss to the tips of her toes. With Buzz holding her tight and his unruly shock of hair tickling her forehead, she felt—for the first time in years—totally secure. Being in his arms was something she would never have dreamed possible after their first hostile meeting. Looking back, she now realized that the hostility was all hers. She intended to make up for that as soon as possible.

"That was very nice," Buzz whispered, when at last their lips parted. "A guy could easily become addicted to kisses like that. I don't suppose you'd happen to have another one on you?"

"You're weird, you know that?" She let him draw her close again, eagerly sharing her second kiss with the man she longed to know better. A lot better.

Chapter Eighteen

Hand in hand, Buzz and Bonnie ambled back toward her house. Before allowing her to enter, however, he searched the entire house again, gun in hand. Without telling Bonnie, he also checked for unpleasant surprises, such as booby-trapped books or kitchen appliances. Survival habits, developed when facing life-or-death situations, died hard. Finding everything in order, he went through the entire house yet again while pointing the antenna of a small black box in all directions. Finding no evidence of listening devices, he invited Bonnie inside.

"This really is a scary mess," Bonnie lamented, scanning the disarray.

"Let me help you get it together. While we do, see if you notice anything missing." The two of them replaced the furniture pieces to their original locations. Then, with Bonnie directing, Buzz returned the paintings to their rightful places. When they'd finished, they worked through the entire house again to make certain they hadn't forgotten to reposition an item of furniture Bonnie might trip on during the night.

"I feel a lot better, now the house is back in order."

"I'm glad. But what you need now is a good night's sleep, and then a fun tomorrow. Have anything planned?"

"Actually, other than exercises with Angela, I haven't given it much thought."

"How about we take Blackie out for a flight at the airfield?"

"I'd like that. As for the invitation, I'd like very much to learn a little more about how you make that guy work."

Buzz grinned like a kid with a new toy, elated by her interest. "Great. What time should I pick you up? I'll have Blackie all loaded and tied down by nine at the latest."

"Okay by me. Nine it is."

Buzz turned toward the door, then turned back when Bonnie said, shyly, "Uh ... I still have one of those kisses left, in case you might be interested in one for the road."

Buzz gently tilted up her chin. "I wouldn't pass up an offer like that for anything." He kissed her tenderly, holding her face in his hands. "Would you mind if I ran my fingers through your hair? I've been wanting to do that ever since you promised not to kill me."

Bonnie pretended to pout. "You're never going to forget about that, are you?"

"Never. It will be the sword of Damocles swinging over your head. Forever."

"Okay, squiggle away." She leaned her head forward for his ministrations, all the while musing how she'd love to have him do much more intimate things than fondle her tresses.

Buzz slowly ran his fingers through Bonnie's hair, savoring her fragrance and the feel of her body against his. She wrapped her arms around his waist and he kissed her forehead, her closed eyes, her nose, and finally her mouth. Their tongues danced. When they held each other more closely, Buzz felt his body beginning to respond to the incredibly pleasant experience. He pulled back. It would be disastrous, he thought, if Bonnie knew the erotic effect she was having on him. *Cripes, I barely know the woman, and something like that might scare hell out of her. She'd probably run like the wind.*

"I'd better get going," he said, his voice husky. "I've got to make a couple of adjustments to Blackie before tomorrow." Noticing Bonnie's frown, he mistakenly guessed she was worried about being alone. "It'll be all right. Nothing further will happen tonight. Just keep your panic button handy."

Bonnie tried to read in bed before falling asleep, but her eyes refused to focus on the words. Her mind kept re-running the bizarre events of the evening, from the moment she entered her violat-

ed house, to the last moment of Buzz's warm embrace. She relived the moment she was certain she
felt a stirring in Buzz's groin, imagining what it
would have been like to grind herself against him.
Would that have ignited his passion and driven
him to run his hands all over her willing body?
No! That would have been stupid. The last thing
she wanted was to scare him away.

The following morning, Bonnie dressed in a
fresh pair of jeans, but was damned if she was going to wear one of her baggy sweatshirts. Maybe
Angela was right—it was time to look more like a
woman. Rummaging in her closet, she selected a
pale pink blouse with long puffed sleeves button-
ing at the wrists. It wasn't a tight-fitting blouse,
but then, it wasn't exactly baggy, either. As she
checked herself in her mirror, Buzz called.

"Oh, hi. I'm all set. Just need to swipe on
some lipstick."

"I'm sorry, Bonnie. But we'll have to change
our plans. I've had a call from David. He's discovered something that will require ... uh, can I come
over and talk to you about this in person?"

"Of course. I'll throw on a pot of coffee. Have
you had breakfast?"

"Just orange juice and an apple."

"I'll fix something. Come when you're ready."

"I'll be there as soon as I collect a few tools."

Tools? Bonnie's curiosity was aroused. What
could David have discovered that required tools on

a Sunday morning—at *her* house? *Oh, well, I suppose I'll soon find out.*

When her doorbell rang fifteen minutes later, she rushed to let him in. On opening the door, she noticed he carried a toolbox in one hand, and two coils of wire in the other.

"I don't remember calling for a telephone repairman," she said.

"Doesn't matter. You need one, and I'm here to do the deed."

"I'm dying to know what's going on, but can you tell me in the kitchen while I pour us some coffee?"

"Sure." He put down his toolbox and wire and followed Bonnie to the kitchen.

After pouring coffee, she put a plate of fresh Danish on the table. "Will this be okay?"

"Uh, do you happen to have a slice of cheese and a piece of fruit? I try to hold down on the sugar."

"Sure." She sliced some Cheddar from a small brick and set out a fresh peach.

"Perfect. By the way, I drink my coffee black, so don't wake the cow."

When they had settled into their food, Bonnie could contain her curiosity no longer. "All right, already. Tell me what's going on."

"You've got to remember that everything I tell you is very confidential. It's like this. When David hacked into Skeeg's computer—"

"He what?"

"He found a way in, and while rummaging through the files he found one labeled 'Bitch.' It turned out to be a list of the harassing tactics he has in mind for you. The dumb shit ... sorry ... doesn't know enough not to put that kind of stuff onto a computer—any computer. He obviously doesn't know it's about as private as e-mail, or a postcard."

"This is incredible."

"Yes. Well, among other things, he eventually plans to break into your house again and destroy some things, after he cuts your phone line."

"That sick sonuvabitch!" Bonnie slammed a fist on the table, jiggling the coffee cups. But anger quickly turned to fear. "What am I gonna *do?*"

"The correct question is, 'What are *we* going to do?'"

"*We?* I already told you, this is *my* problem." She wondered what her brothers would think if they knew she'd abdicated control to a stranger.

Buzz looked directly into Bonnie's blue eyes. Softly, he said, "No, we agreed it's *our* problem. And the first thing to do is fix your phone line so that Skeegy-boy won't be able to cut it."

"How can you do that?"

"I'm going to re-route your real line and put a dummy line in its place. That way, when he cuts a line, he'll cut the dummy."

"Oh."

"But when he cuts the dummy line, he'll also set off an alarm that'll sound all over my house."

"Why not make it sound outside? Maybe that would scare him away?"

"We don't want to scare him away just so he can come back another day. We want to get him off your back for good. If the alarm rings at my house, that'll give me time to respond before he gets into the house."

"And just what do you imagine *me* doing while this is going on?"

"Depends on when it happens and where you are. We can talk about that later." He collected his tools and wire, and went outside to put his plan into action.

By lunchtime he'd accomplished his mission, and Bonnie willingly helped him test the new arrangement. Sure enough, it did what it was supposed to do, and she was pleased at finally having been given some part to play in the process.

"The least I can do is offer you some lunch," she said. "How about a roast beef sandwich and beer?"

"Sounds great. Not that I'm hungry or anything. I probably couldn't eat more than *half* a cow."

Buzz dug into his lunch with enthusiasm. After he'd wolfed down a large sandwich and two bottles of beer, Bonnie placed an apple pie on the table.

"Gee, that smells good. Where do you get such terrific pastry?"

"I make it."

"Really?"

Bonnie sliced a large piece and, placing it on a plate, put it in front of Buzz. "Yes, really! Living alone, I don't bake often, but I like to exercise my cooking skills whenever there's an excuse."

"Where'd you learn to cook so well?"

"My father's an Army officer, and after my brothers graduated and moved out, and my mother died, I cooked for the two of us whenever he came home on furlough."

"You know, if you ever decide to take in boarders, I'd like to apply for a seat at your table."

Bonnie thought that would be very nice, especially if Buzz were the only boarder.

Looking at his watch, Buzz stood. "I think I'd better go. We need to do some plotting before you start mining for information tomorrow."

"What do you mean *we,* White Man?"

"David and I."

"What about me? This is *my* problem, in case you've forgotten."

"I haven't forgotten," Buzz said. "But you're going to have your hands full on Monday doing your part in the information-gathering department. After that, you'll have to lie low for a few days and let us do what we have to do, after—"

"No." Her fist pounded the table to emphasize

the word. "This is *my* problem and I will not play helpless female while the macho male hunters go off to slay the dragon. And that's final."

Buzz stared open-mouthed at Bonnie, but said nothing. He thought she'd already agreed to accept his help. He admired her determination to participate in "slaying the dragon," as she put it, but the situation was far more dangerous than she realized.

"Bonnie, I really admire your spunk, and your determination to deal with the problem yourself. You are one terrific woman. But let me see if I can explain why we need you to participate during the next few days by hardly participating at all."

Belligerently, she put her hands on her hips. "Yeah, lemme see you explain it."

"All right. During the first few days things will be happening to Skeeg mainly at the office. When they do, he'll immediately suspect *you* as the doer. If you know what we're planning, or when it's going to happen, there's no way you'll be able to act surprised and innocent."

"And why not, if I may ask?"

"Because you haven't been trained to lie."

Bonnie thought about that for a moment, then slowly nodded, having realized the truth of the comment. She hadn't had any training at all in deception. Worse, she remembered her father telling her she was a lousy liar on those rare occasions she tried to slip something past him.

"Look, Bonnie. Skeeg is going to be pretty up-set at what happens to him. If you give any indica-tion at all that you know something about it, he'll land on you like a ton of bricks. None of us wants that."

"So I just sit here and twiddle my thumbs?"

"Not quite. We've already agreed that tomor-row you'll discreetly collect some vital information, *then* you'll lie low. I promise, when the time is right, we'll plug you into the action."

"Promise?"

"Promise. We have to be sure we don't put you in harm's way. Skeeg is going to continue to escalate, don't forget."

"I can take care of Skeegy-scumbag if I have to."

"Indeed, you can. But if he escalates to using weapons, don't forget that a gun trumps martial arts."

"And you just happen to have one, I've no-ticed."

"Along with a permit from the State of Arizona to carry it concealed. We don't really need permits any more, but I like to keep my skills sharp."

This man keeps getting more and more com-plicated—and interesting. Just as I think I've seen the limit of his skills, another one surfaces. I just hope I'll have a chance to explore the far corners of his mind. She imagined herself and Buzz curled up on a couch, her head on his shoulder as he recounted the mysterious adventures of his life.

"Bonnie?"

"Yes?" Her fantasy interrupted, she dragged her brain back to the present.

"A final reminder. Be very careful tomorrow when you look for information. One slip and you could blow the entire plan and put yourself in real danger."

Chapter Nineteen

Bonnie's Monday was like no other she'd ever experienced. She rose early to allow careful preparation for the intriguing information-collection assignment ahead. Imagining herself as "Bonnie, Super-Spy," deftly ferreting information from under the noses of the unsuspecting; "Bonnie the Magician," causing information to disappear while remaining in plain sight; and "Bonnie the Avenger," fighting evil wherever it appeared. It was a heady feeling to realize she at last would have an active part in the action. The sense of anticipation made her eyes gleam and her nerve endings tingle. This day would be anything but routine.

She refilled Fang's water and food dishes, providing adequate sustenance for the day.

Fang chirped, seemingly pleased at Bonnie's upbeat mood. "And," she explained, "knowing that sleazeball Skeeg is behind the office fiascos, I won't have to tear my hair out trying to solve the mystery."

Fang tweeted his approval.

"Furthermore," she added, "I will be the essence of discretion. Sherlock Holmes would be proud."

Bonnie washed and dried her breakfast dishes, retouched her makeup, then studied herself once more in the mirror. Then, with a purposeful stride, she headed out toward the adventures that awaited.

*   *   *

"Wow," Felina exclaimed when Bonnie entered the office. "Don't *you* look spiffy. That bright yellow blouse really contrasts well with your dark suit. Something special happen over the weekend?"

"If you call a good night's sleep special, then absolutely yes!   How're you two coming with the rewrites?"

"Okay," Amalina responded. "A little slower than we'd planned, but we'll meet your deadline."

The chit-chat continued until the agenda for the day had been settled. When her associates appeared occupied with their work, Bonnie excused herself and stepped out of the office. Armed with Skeeg's license number, she headed straight for the parking garage in the basement, slowly walking up and down the rows of cars until she found the black BMW. "There you are," she murmured, and made a note of the exact location of the car. It occurred to her that as the space wasn't marked with Skeeg's name, there was no guarantee the car would be parked in the same spot tomorrow. No matter. She'd just tell the guys what she had learned. They could take it from there.

Next, she set out to record the exact location of Skeeg's office in relation to doors and other landmarks. Carrying a clipboard, she walked from her office toward Skeeg's, noting the number of steps. She made note of several features, and was amazed at how many things had been invisible until she actually looked.

She found a fire extinguisher in each hallway, surprised to note they weren't all the same size. She found a maintenance closet next to the ladies' room, but where was the men's room? She didn't find it until she'd walked halfway around the building. After noting several other features on her list, she was convinced she could now describe the location of both her and Skeeg's offices with great accuracy.

During the remainder of the morning she collected the other items of information David Chin had asked her to assemble, crossing off each item in turn. She was relieved not to have to sneak into Skeeg's office to collect ID information about his computer. After all, if Chin had already hacked into it, he must already have that.

Later, returning from lunch, Bonnie found Felina and Amalina gushing over a huge flower arrangement just delivered to their office.

"The delivery guy said it's for you, Bonnie. Open the card," Amalina urged. "Who's it from?"

Bonnie took the card from the small envelope and read:

From me to me.
Bonnie

"You sent these flowers to *yourself?* What a weird idea."

"I did *not* send these flowers to myself," Bonnie retorted, immediately wishing she could erase the words from the air. What could she say, without letting the Skeeg story out of the bag? She was going to have to learn to think before speaking, she told herself.

"Well," she stammered, "I did, and I didn't."

Felina put a hand over her mouth, but couldn't prevent a giggle from escaping. "Don't y'all just love it when she talks like that?"

"What I mean is ... uh ... they're for my house. I couldn't have them delivered there, because no one's home. So I had them dropped off here. I just thought I'd brighten up my place a little." *Now, how am I going to get this huge bunch of flowers into my little Honda without smashing them?* she wondered.

"Boy, those must have cost you a bundle."

Bonnie's eyes widened as she realized Skeeg

must have given the florist her name, office address, and home phone number, and that the flowers would be billed to *her*. *Why, that low-down,
sleazy sonuvabitch.* A moment later, a small smile
tinged the edges of her lips as she remembered the
plan being hatched by David and Buzz. *Yes,* she
decided, *I can tolerate a little harassment—it
won't be for long.*

As she left the building later that afternoon
with the large bouquet of flowers, Bonnie remembered one assigned task she'd left undone. Her
body tensed as the thought of sneaking into anybody's office and stealing the contents of a wastebasket. It didn't seem like much of a transgres-
sion, but her strong sense of honesty caused her to
hang back. She hadn't done anything wrong, yet
she already felt like a criminal. *Dad was right:
I'm lousy at deception.* Finally, she decided to
skip the wastebasket-pilfering task and report her
findings to Buzz. Just thinking about Buzz
warmed her, sending small tendrils of excitement
along long-unused pathways of her nervous system.

Before entering her house, she placed the bouquet on the porch floor and walked around to the
back to check the water faucet for running water.
She continued checking the exterior, then retrieved the bouquet and entered the house. Even
before hunting for a suitable container for the
flowers, she walked through the entire house, ex-

pecting to discover more mischief committed by
Skeeg. When nothing seemed amiss, she re-
supplied Fang's food and water supplies.

"Now then," she said to Fang, "what the heck
have I got that's big enough to hold all these flowers?" Her hunt revealed nothing large enough to
contain the entire bouquet, so she broke it into
smaller segments and spread those throughout the
house.

Now it was time to call Buzz and make her report. When he came on the line, she said, "Hello?
Is this Spy Central?"

"I'm afraid you've got the wrong number,
lady," he said, immediately falling in with Bonnie's
gag. "You've reached Smooch-Starved, International.

Bonnie laughed. "You're quick on the uptake,
aren't you, Buzz?"

"Yeah, I try to be on my toes when I hear your
voice. Never know when you're planning to kill me
again, you know."

"You're never gonna let go of that, are you?"
she said.

"Not a chance. I have to remain vigilant at all
times. My virginity is at stake here, you know."

Bonnie laughed again. "No, I didn't know.
Now then, if you can come over here I will spill the
beans and share my mountain of brand-new intelligence."

"Done," he said. "Ten minutes."

Exactly ten minutes later, Bonnie's doorbell rang. She cracked open the door and said, "What's the secret password?"

"Uh ... a hug and a kiss?"

"That's it," she replied, opening the door wide. She flung her arms around his neck and kissed him soundly. "There. Now you can come in."

"Wow! Where'd you get all the pretty flowers?" Buzz asked as he stepped through the foyer into the kitchen.

"I'll tell you the sordid story as soon as I've poured us something of a liquid persuasion. What would you like?"

"A beer would be nice," he said.

She got Buzz the beer, and poured a glass of orange juice for herself. She then gave Buzz the notes she'd written during the day. "One thing that isn't in my notes is anything about these flowers. I don't have any proof, but I'm certain that S.O.B., Skeeg, ordered them in *my* name, so *I'm* going to have to pay for them."

Buzz snickered. "I've never heard of that one before. I'll have to tell David." After reviewing her notes, he said, "It looks as if you've collected a lot of information in very little time. Nice work!"

"But I'm ashamed of myself for not having the nerve to sneak into Skeeg's office to take papers from his wastebasket."

"That's okay. Don't worry about it."

"Actually, I got all shaky just thinking about it.

I'm beginning to see the wisdom of your decision to keep me in the dark for awhile."

"Don't beat yourself up. You haven't had any training in this sort of thing, so your feelings are those of an upstanding, honest citizen."

"I don't *care*. I want to do something to get this creep off my back."

"You will—I promise. Actually, you've already begun," he said, waving her notes in the air.

Those softly spoken words reassured Bonnie, and she relaxed. Somehow, she thought, Buzz always knew the right thing to say to make her feel warm and comfortable. She wondered whether the word "relationship" could be used to describe their growing friendship. If so, there was still an unknown something holding them apart. Sure, they were polite in one another's company, and they kissed on occasion, but every time it seemed that it might turn into a "relationship between lovers," it suddenly morphed into something more like a "relationship between siblings—or co-conspirators." Remembering the day Buzz repaired her torn dress-strap, she longed for the day he would rip it from her body and ravish her from head to toe. *That may be a long time coming,* she thought gloomily. *Why, he hasn't even asked me for an ordinary date.*

"What was Skeeg like today?" Buzz asked.

"We hardly saw him. He's working on some kind of report to give his boss tomorrow morning.

Mr. Nesbitt told him to summarize what he's learned about our project since their last meeting. At least, that's what his secretary told me. So, other than popping in for copies of some of our reports, we haven't seen him at all."

"That's great!"

"Why is it great?"

"Um ... I can't tell you. Just stay tuned." Buzz stood and paced, obviously deep in thought. Turning toward Bonnie, he said, "Much as I hate to do this, may I cut this short? I think I'd better spend some serious time with David."

"Was it something I said?" Another lost opportunity to spend time with Buzz, and delight him with her feminine charms. *Damn!*

"Actually, it was. But you didn't say anything wrong, if that's what you're thinking."

It was exactly what I was thinking, and how did he know that? Did he learn mind-reading in spy school, too? "That *is* what I was thinking, and I'm glad I was wrong."

Buzz moved closer and, putting his hands on her arms, said, "I'm really sorry, but what you just told me needs to get to David right away. Before I go, though, I ... uh ... I don't suppose you have another of those kisses left over from yesterday, do you? Those seem to have worn off."

Bonnie eased her body against his and wrapped her arms around his waist. "It just so happens you're in luck. Try this one on for size."

With that, she took hold of his ears and pulled his head to hers. As his strong arms enveloped her, his masculine fragrance and after-shave lotion overwhelmed her. *Why,* she asked herself, *was he shaving so late in the day? For me?* Then she wondered why she gave a damn about his shaving habits, concentrating, instead, on the erotic pleasures her aroused body was experiencing. She held him tightly, and let her fingernails lightly scratch the back of his neck. Just as she felt a bulge growing in his jeans, he backed away ... just like the last time. She wondered what she had done wrong.

Buzz, with Bonnie's firm, full breasts hard against his chest, her tongue dancing in his mouth, wanted desperately to make love to this warm, apparently willing, woman. Right here and now! He wanted to pick her up, carry her masterfully to the bedroom, fling her onto the bed and plunge himself into her luscious body. But he didn't! As soon as he felt himself hardening, he pulled away. He couldn't stop himself; it just happened.

"You were right." He waved his arms for emphasis as he spoke, hoping it would distract her from noticing his growing erection. "That was one of your better-class kisses. I hope I didn't use up your last one."

"Not a chance," she said. "Actually, I come fully equipped with a lifetime supply." *Darn! Why doesn't he pick up on that invitation to smother me with kisses? Am I that unattractive?*

"Wonderful! Save some for me, will you? But I've really got to get on-line with David. You've done a great job today and he's gonna be thrilled with what you've discovered."

"I'm glad you're pleased."

"Look, Bonnie, I really would like to stay. But—"

"I understand. Go, already. And ... keep in touch."

"You can bet on it."

Bonnie was struck by a sudden thought.

"Uh, Buzz?"

"Yes?"

"If you're going to call David, could you ask him if Skeeg emailed a José Barraloza in Mexico City during the past three days, and what the content of the message was?" She recited the email address.

"Sure. What's that about?"

"Tell you later. Right now it's *my* turn to be mysterious."

*   *   *

Buzz waved his fingers over his keyboard. As soon as he was sure of their encryption connection, he filled David in on the information Bonnie had collected during the day.

"That's good stuff, Ram—or should I call you Buzz?"

"Cut the crap! Here's the best part." Buzz told him about the summary report Skeeg was supposed to have ready for Court Nesbitt the following morning, and about the e-mail Bonnie wanted him to check on.

"Nice work. We can use that right now. Let's change our agenda and put that report on top of our list. Okay with you?"

"Fine. Let me know if there's something I can do."

"I don't suppose Bonnie knew the filename?"

"She didn't say. I doubt it."

"No problem. I'll get on that and the email right now. See 'ya."

*   *   *

The following morning Skeeg responded to a summons from Court Nesbitt.

"Come in and sit down, Bart." Nesbitt stood at his stand-up desk and waited, deliberately giving Skeeg time to sit and worry about the purpose of the meeting. Finally, he joined Skeeg at the coffee table in the corner of his office.

"Have you finished the project summary I asked you for?"

Nesbitt noticed Skeeg had arrived empty-handed, and waited for the inevitable excuse. Though he'd already given Skeeg his last warning, he would add this latest lapse to the log wherein he documented Skeeg's failures to perform.

"That's just it," Skeeg began, frowning and wringing his hands. "I had it all done. When I came in this morning to print it out, it was *gone*."

"Gone?"

"Gone. I had it in a file labeled 'Sales Project,' but it just isn't there anymore." Skeeg squirmed in his chair, his frown deepening.

"In other words, the dog ate your homework, eh? I don't suppose you remembered to back up your file?"

Skeeg's rapidly moving eyes met Nesbitt's steady stare. "Of *course* I backed it up. I keep a back-up file on my hard drive and also on an external drive, and back up everything before I go home. Every day. But *that's* gone, too. I even got somebody from Computer Services to come up and try to find it—"

"But it's still gone. Right?"

"I honest-to-God don't know how it could have happened. I've never lost a file before. Not from my computer."

"Uh-huh." Nesbitt stood. "Well, if you ever find it, let me know. In the meantime, you might try a little harder." He walked toward his desk, signaling the end of the meeting.

Skeeg stood. As he headed for the door, he turned and said, "Look, Mr. Nesbitt. I'm really sorry. I had it all done, and then the damn file just *disappeared*. I ... I really didn't screw up. It's just that ... well, I don't know *what* happened."

"As I said, if you ever find it, let me know."

Skeeg couldn't think of anything else to say, and turned to leave. Visibly shaken by this unexpected source of frustration, he slowly wandered toward Bonnie's office while thinking about this strange mystery. He was certain he'd completed the report, and he remembered backing it up before leaving. Where the hell could it have gone?

He found himself standing in Bonnie's office, still deep in thought.

"Can we help you with something?" Bonnie asked.

"Yes. I need to borrow those files again ... the ones you lent me last week. Okay?"

"Are you all right? You look rattled."

"Uh ... it's okay. I just need to borrow those files again."

"Sure. Anything else?" She paused. "You sure you're all right?"

"No, goddammit, I'm *not* all right," Skeeg blurted, flinging his arms into the air.

Felina and Amalina raised their heads from their charts at the sudden explosion of emotion.

"I had my project report all ready to print out, and it *just disappeared.*"

"From your computer?"

"Of course, from my computer."

"It's not on your back-up disk?"

"It's gone from there, too, and I don't know

what the hell happened."

"I'm sorry."

"Look. Just give me those files and I'll get 'em back to you as soon as I can."

Wow, Bonnie chuckled inwardly, *they've started. They've hacked into his computer again and wiped out his report file.* Certain it was David Chin who'd deleted the files, she turned away to keep Skeeg from seeing her uncontrollable smile. "I'll get the files right now," she managed to say. She was elated. *This will have to take his mind off his stalking activities, at least for a little while.*

When Skeeg left with the files, Bonnie called Buzz from a phone in an empty conference room.

"Mister Skeeg seems to be missing a file from his computer."

"I wonder how that could have happened?"

"Oh, and don't *you* sound smug? I'll bet there's a little halo around your head right now, too, isn't there?"

"If there is, there should be one around your own as well. After all, you made it possible. Stay tuned."

Chapter Twenty

"David, old friend, you are one effin' genius!" The encrypted line crackled with Buzz's sounds of elation.

"Oh? Whut'd I do?"

"Don't play the innocent with me, you old fart. Bonnie called to tell me Skeeg's lost an important file from his computer and back-up drive."

"Serves 'im right for leaving his external back-up drive connected. Dumb, dumb, dumb."

"Right. Anything on the Barraloza e-mail?

"Nope. Not a word."

"Thanks. I'll pass that along to Bonnie. What's next on the agenda?"

"Skeeg seems to have a lot of junk on his hard drive," David said. "Not much in the way of important stuff, so I thought it might be fun to switch the folder and file names on some of them. What do you think?"

"Sounds good. When he opens a file labeled 'Finances,' or something, he'll get the contents of one labeled 'Favorite Recipes.' That'll rattle his cage. Do it."

"OK. I've got an even nastier one for later in the week—how about I copy his stalking file to his boss's computer, and maybe a couple others as well?"

"Terrific," Buzz said. "But yeah, let's wait with that one 'til later in the week. By then he should be ready to blow."

"You ready with your action items?"

"Got one planned for this afternoon. I'll be in touch."

*   *   *

Dressed to blend in with the Marsden-style business-wear Bonnie had described—slacks, jacket, no tie—Buzz parked in a Visitor's space at Marsden Manufacturing, and made his way to the rear of the parking lot and the underground ramp. Without a company identity badge, he needed to be careful not to have his presence challenged. Glancing about to make sure no one was at the entrance, he walked into the garage and down the ramp to the first level of cars. Skeeg's car should be one level below. He located the stairs to the lower level and walked toward them. So far, so good.

As he reached the bottom stair, he spotted a woman walking in his direction. Quickly, he moved in the opposite direction to conceal his face.

When he'd guessed the woman had started up the stairs, he turned and began his search for Skeeg's car. It wasn't hard to find—it was right where Bonnie said it would be. He stooped beside the left front wheel and removed an item from his pocket. Ten seconds later, he stood and scanned the area. Seeing no one approaching, he retraced his steps to the Visitors' area and to his car. Mission accomplished. Noting the time—2:35 pm—he drove home.

*   *   *

"Buzz, it's Bonnie."

"I recognized the dulcet tones."

"Have you had dinner yet? I've a roast in the oven that I can't eat all by myself. Wanna share it?"

"That'd be marvelous! All I've got in my fridge is a hank of hair and a piece of baling wire."

Bonnie laughed. "Come whenever you're ready."

"Will do, and thanks for the invitation." He paused. "Oh, wait."

"What?"

"There's one condition ... no, two."

"What are they?"

"First off, you have to promise you won't pump me for information about what's going on."

"Damn! That shoots my agenda all to heck.

I'm dying to know what the next move will be."

"Sorry. There's one thing I *can* tell you, though—but you'll have to play it cool in the office. Promise?"

"Promise."

"Skeeg never sent that e-mail you asked about."

"Why am I not surprised? Well, I'll just have to deal with it myself. Okay, what's your other condition?"

"I'll have to head for home after dinner. The neighbor kids are coming over to work on their model planes around seven-thirty. The kids are so eager to get their planes into the air they've pestered their parents to convince me to set up an extra session."

"I thought they came on week-ends."

"They do. But they're so close to having their planes ready to fly, they can taste it. They begged me, so I said to come ahead. Okay?"

"I guess so." Bonnie's voice revealed her disappointment. She'd planned to demonstrate her culinary skill with dinner and wine, then share a quiet evening with Buzz. She should have known better. *Oh, well, half a loaf* ....

The roast, surrounded by glazed carrots and mashed potatoes, preceded by a tossed green salad, was a huge success. Buzz couldn't rave about it enough. "Y'know," he said, "I don't get around much socially, but I can't remember meeting a woman who actually knew how to cook anything as tasty as this dinner."

"Thank you."

"And the wine added just the right touch. If I didn't have to be stone cold sober when I get home, I'd finish the bottle ... or try to." Buzz lifted his wine glass in a toast. "You are a very talented woman, and I'm proud and lucky to have you as a neighbor."

More! she thought. *More! Tell me more. What about* me? *Don't you* like *me? Don't you want to wrap your arms around me, and kiss me, and carry me off to bed? What am I doing wrong?*

Buzz helped clear the dishes from the table. "Now what's this mysterious e-mail business about?"

Bonnie filled him in, and added, "I can fix this one. I'll just call Barraloza and pass on the message myself. Skeeg won't know anything about it."

"Sounds good. And now, dear lady," he announced, "there's something I want you to have." Hurrying to the front door, he retrieved an old Roi Tan cigar box he'd left on the empty umbrella stand on his arrival. Handing it to Bonnie, he proudly announced, "I want you to have this."

Bonnie wasn't sure what to make of his gesture. A joke? No, his tone of voice ruled that out.

"What is it?"

"It's the very first model airplane I ever made."

Bonnie opened the box and took out the small yellow airplane.

"It's a Sopwith Camel," he said. "Just like the one Snoopy flies."

"My God!" Bonnie said, tears forming in her eyes. "This is one of your boyhood treasures, and you want *me* to have it? It's beautiful," she managed to add, turning the object this way and that, stroking it gently with her fingers. "You must have worked very hard on it." She couldn't have known, but that was exactly the right thing to say.

"I want you to keep it."

"Thank you. It's very thoughtful. I'll find just the place to display it, and when someone asks me about it, I'll tell them it was a gift from someone very special."

Buzz smiled, as pleased as a youngster bringing his first clay ash tray home to his mother.

His gesture reminded her of a small boy trying to impress a little girl by giving her his most treasured dead lizard. It was sweet beyond description.

"Now I have to run."

"Not before I express my appreciation for your gift." She leaped up and wrapped her arms around his neck, and pulled his head to hers for a short embrace. The only sound was the music playing in her soul.

"Y'know," Buzz mumbled, "if you're not careful, I could get addicted to your touch."

"I wouldn't mind."

Fang chirped agreement from his cage.

"Mmm ... I'll have to think about that." He smiled. "Oh, by the way, you won't have to worry about Skeeg tonight."

"Why not?"

"He'll be much too busy."

Chapter Twenty-One

The following morning, Skeeg stormed into his office an hour late. "Brenda, get in here!"

"Gee, you don't need to shout. Something wrong?"

"Yes, dammit! Something's wrong." Skeeg paced as he ranted. "When I left to go home last night, one of my tires was flat and I couldn't change it—no jack. Took me two hours to get a tow truck into the garage, and *another* two hours to get the damned tire fixed. I never made it to my dinner appointment."

"I'm sorry."

"If it isn't one thing, it's another. It's as though I've suddenly been jinxed."

"Is there anything I can do?"

"Yes. You can take a memo to Building Maintenance." Skeeg dictated a scathing memo complaining about the large nail found in his tire, blaming it on sloppy cleaning of the garage floors.

"You sure you want to send this?" Brenda knew the invective-laden memo would cause the grapevine to go nuts.

"*Yes, dammit! Send it now!*" Skeeg was so upset by this new incident he found it difficult to concentrate on reconstructing his missing report. He'd have been even more upset had he known another visit was being paid to his car at that very moment.

I've just got to complete that report, he told himself. I gotta redeem myself with Nesbitt. He's pissed at me for not getting it to him when he expected it, and I know damn well he didn't believe a word I said when I told him it just plain disappeared from my computer. Suddenly my world is coming all unglued ... and dammit, it's not my fault! He paced from one end of his office to the other for some time before again trying to tackle the report.

*   *   *

Skeeg noticed the flashing red and yellow lights on his way home. *Why the hell doesn't the dumb cop just go around me?* he wondered. *There's a whole empty lane to my left.* Finally, it dawned on him that *he* was the target of the flashing lights. Steaming, he pulled to the curb and stopped. "*Now* what," he blurted, banging his hands on the steering wheel.

The police officer seemed to be ambling toward him in slow motion.

Skeeg sat and fumed, his hands clenching the steering wheel. A knock on the window, and Skeeg lowered it.

"Good afternoon, sir. May I see your license and registration, please?"

Skeeg disconnected his seatbelt to reach his wallet, handed his driver's license to the officer, and rummaged through the glove compartment to locate his registration.

"Did you know you're driving on a public street without a license plate?"

"*What?* That's crazy!" Skeeg tried to get out to look for himself, but the police officer blocked his exit.

"If you'll just follow me, please, I'll lead you to the nearest DMV office. You can fill out the forms for a plate replacement."

"*Jeesus!*" Skeeg slammed the steering wheel with both hands. "Can't I just do that in the morning? I'm on my way to meet someone. I thought you were just supposed to give me a ticket."

"Yes, sir. But if I let you drive without a plate, you'll just be stopped by every patrol that notices. You'll save yourself a lot of time and grief if you simply follow me now." The officer turned to go back to his patrol car, its light bar still flashing.

Skeeg was no stranger to things going wrong on occasion, but this was unheard of. No, it was outrageous! He'd never been so frustrated and humiliated in his entire life. Not even when his father berated him for being a stupid, lazy oaf who would never amount to anything. But, seeing no alternative, he followed the police car to the closest DMV office and parked.

On entering the large room, Skeeg approached the receptionist's desk. She instructed him to take a number from its red dispenser and wait until called. With the numbered ticket, driver's license, and registration in hand, he found a seat and waited. And waited ... and waited.

Twenty minutes later he heard his number called. Directed to counter 17, where the clerk was counting a large stack of completed forms, he tried to state his problem.

"I've got to get a—"

A wave of the clerk's hand told him he should wait until she finished counting. Shifting his weight from one foot to the other, then back again, he waited some more. When at last she finished the count, she looked up and turned her attention to Skeeg.

"I'm sorry, but we're just closing for the day. You'll have to come back tomorrow."

That was more than Skeeg could bear. He slammed an open hand on the counter, causing all heads to turn in his direction. "You *can't* close *now*," he shouted. "I've been waiting here forever to get a temporary license plate, and I need it now. I just got a ticket for not having a plate and—"

"Well, you should have applied for a replacement as soon as you lost it." While she spoke, she pressed the alarm button mounted under the counter.

"I *am* applying as soon as I lost—as soon as I found out it was gone."

"Well, it's closing time and—"

"I don't give a damn if it is closing time. That cop who sent me here didn't tell me it would be closing time, or that I would run into any trouble. I need a plate *now!*" He pounded on the counter. "Is that too much to ask? I can't leave here without it!" Skeeg shouted and banged his hand on the counter again.

"I'm sorry, but there's nothing I can do."

Suddenly a pair of security guards materialized at his sides.

"Sir, you're making a disturbance. We'll have to ask you to come with us." They took him by the arms and propelled him toward a security booth at the end of the hall.

Skeeg squirmed and tried to get them to release their hold. "Let me go, dammit. I'm just trying to get a temporary plate so I can drive home ... and that ... that damned *bureaucrat* tried to stop me."

"She was just doing her job, sir. Now try to calm down."

"Oh, that's great. That's just great! I should calm down when all I want is a little service from our civil servants. I'm a taxpayer, you know. And it's not as if I just showed up at closing time—they kept me waiting forever only to slam the door in my face!" Beads of sweat formed on his brow and his face contorted in rage. "How the hell do you expect me to get home if I don't have a plate?"

"That's being taken care of, sir. We've a car waiting outside."

When he was propelled from the building, Skeeg exploded anew. "A *police* car? Are you *nuts?* What will my neighbors think?"

"We can call you a cab, if you prefer."

*   *   *

Skeeg stomped into his office a little after ten the following morning and booted his computer with jabbing fingers. Still upset over the events of the day before, he scanned for e-mails and was grateful for the absence of any requiring immediate reply. Pleased, but puzzled, over the absence of messages, he next set out to complete his reconstruction of the mysteriously vanishing report. But he couldn't find the folder. Anywhere. He opened every folder and scanned every file. It was gone. Again! Worse, filenames didn't match their contents. When he tried to open his "Bitch" file, a tax spreadsheet blossomed on his screen. When he opened his "Bonnie Project" file, it came up empty, except for a paragraph of type too small to read with the naked eye. The contents of every folder seemed to have been interchanged with the contents of another. *What the hell is going on?*

"This isn't *possible*," Skeeg shouted, slamming his fists on his desk. "Damned computers!"

Alarmed at the outburst, Brenda got up from her station and came to his door. "What's wrong now?"

"I can't find the damn report folder again. I can find the *folder*, but it's empty. And every other folder is mixed up with the contents of some other damned folder. Have you been messing with my machine?"

"Certainly not. I never touch it."

"Well then, this computer has turned into a piece of shit."

"You lost the same one that disappeared before?"

"I just told you that. What are you, *deaf?* Yes, the one that disappeared before. I had it almost re-done, now it's gone again. Nesbitt's gonna kill me."

"Can I do anything to help?"

"You can go borrow those files back from Bonnie. I'll just have to start all over again." Brenda left, and Skeeg sat down hard to open a new project file on his un-cooperative computer.

A smiling Bonnie finished a satisfying phone conversation with José Barraloza, who had leaped at the chance to participate in the upcoming project tryout. As she completed the call, her other phone rang. It was Brenda.

"Hi, Bonnie. Bart lost the file again from his computer."

"Oh?" That's what she said. In her mind, she rejoiced. *Aha! The Buzz Boys strike again!*

"Yeah. The same one that disappeared yesterday. And he said all the other folders have had their contents switched. He's not in a good mood right now. Though this time, I really can't blame him—there's nothing like a computer mess to drive you out of your skull. Anyway, he's in about as foul a mood as I've ever seen, so I'd avoid him if you can. He's trying to start writing that report all over again ... for the third time. Can I borrow those files again?"

"Sure." Bonnie moved to collect the requested folders. "How'd it get lost again?"

"He doesn't have any idea, and it's driving him crazy. But there's more." Brenda described Skeeg's late arrival, and told her about Skeeg's being stopped for not having a license plate. "Then he couldn't get one at the DMV because they were closing, so they drove him home in a police car, and he had to take a cab over there again this morning. That's why he was late again."

Bonnie tried to keep the muscles of her mouth from forming into a satisfied smile. She barely succeeded.

"Maybe he needs to have his computer repaired."

"Yeah. Maybe. I think he's about ready to slam his fist through the screen."

During her drive home that afternoon, Bonnie mulled the recent events. Buzz and David are taking all the risk, and having all the fun. But it's *my* problem, after all, and I'm not going to sit on the sidelines any longer. I've got to do *something,* with or without their blessing.

She recognized the recklessness of her decision, but was determined not to be just an idle bystander. Collecting information had apparently been useful, but not enough. Action—*any* kind of action, would make her feel whole again.

Bonnie began her campaign by putting fresh newspaper in the bottom of Fang's cage. "There, sweetie-bird. Now you can read the latest comics." After a cheese sandwich and a glass of milk, she set about making her own list of attack items. But after half an hour of serious thought, she had only two items on her list.

"This is harder than I thought," she told Fang. "I'm just not very good at this clandestine stuff. But, dammit, I'll go bonkers if I don't do *something!*"

She forced herself again to concentrate, and this time it wasn't long before she had a germ of an idea. The germ grew into a plan, and the very existence of the plan strengthened her determination. Turning it over in her mind, she couldn't find a flaw. "That's it!" she exulted, and ran to her bed-

room to change clothes. Once dressed in black
running attire, she drove to the Pep Boys automo-
tive supply store and made two small purchases.
Returning to her car, she rummaged in her purse
for the slip of paper with Skeeg's home address
scrawled on it, along with a roughly-drawn map.

The address turned out to be a single-story
condo on the west side of Phoenix. Bonnie drove
by the address slowly, then turned around to park
across the street. Removing a small pair of opera
glasses from her purse, she scanned the property
to familiarize herself with its features. Though a
street light glowed several doors away, Skeeg's
front door remained in relative darkness. That,
and the potted plants and trees dotting the driveway, provided some concealment for what she was
planning to do. Skeeg's car parked in the carport
suggested he must be home. But the condo was
dark, so she concluded he must be asleep. So far,
so good.

Her heart pounding and her palms moist, Bonnie stepped out of the car. Leaving it unlocked,
she sauntered casually across the street, steeling
herself not to look left and right, as she thought a
burglar might. Moving directly to the front door,
she gave the lock a quick "treatment." She then
made a short stop at Skeeg's car. Finally, returning to her own car, she drove off.

Only when she'd entered the freeway heading
north did she let out the breath she hadn't realized

she was holding. Inhaling deeply several times, she felt her apprehension morph into exhilaration. She could hardly wait to tell Buzz. She hoped her hands would stop shaking by then.

"Buzz, it's Bonnie."

"Hi. Hold on a sec. I'm on line with David ... let me tell him I'll call him back."

"No, wait. If it's okay to come over, I've got something to tell both of you."

"Okay, come ahead. I'll unlock the front door. You know where I'll be."

A few minutes later an ebullient Bonnie walked into Buzz's den, where he and David were talking on the encrypted line.

"Bonnie's here," Buzz said to his computer.

"Yes, I can see her. Hi, Bonnie."

"Hi, David. I've got something to tell you both."

"What is it?" This from David.

Beaming with pride at her initiative, Bonnie described her escapade at Skeeg's front door.

"You did *what?*" Buzz and David exclaimed, almost in unison.

"As I said. I squirted his front door lock with superglue. It should have hardened in seconds."

"My God, Bonnie, do you realize what you've *done?*" Buzz shot out of his chair and began pacing, a deep scowl on his face.

"What I've *done,*" said Bonnie, suddenly on the defensive, "is finally take some action myself on *my* problem."

"No!" Buzz shot back, jabbing a finger in Bonnie's direction. "What you've *done* is tell Skeeg that somebody is doing all the things that until *now* he believed was a lousy run of bad luck. What you've done is let him know he's a *target,* which he *didn't* know, or couldn't be sure of, until now. Jeezus, Bonnie, what were you *thinking?*"

"He could think it was just some kids or vandals—"

"Not a chance. With everything that's been happening to him, his first thought will be to wonder who has been targeting him, and guess who he's gonna think of *first? You!*"

"I don't *care,*" Bonnie shot back, her voice rising. "I'm tired of sitting around doing nothing. Besides, you promised me a part of the action and you haven't done anything to keep that promise except have me collect a little information."

"Oh, that's just great!" Buzz responded. "*You're* tired of sitting around, so to massage your ego you decide to risk the entire operation, and your *life* as well." Slowly, he shook his head, wondering what he ever saw in this crazy woman.

Bonnie's shoulders sagged and her face fell. "I'm ... I'm sorry. I guess I didn't think of that."

"Obviously. Why do you think David and I asked you to butt out for a few days? It's exactly because we didn't want something like this to happen."

"I'm sorry. I really am. I just thought I could
... I was so *sure* my plan was foolproof."

David joined the conversation. "Ram, we're
going to have to compress our timetable now."

"Right."

"And you're gonna have to do some damage
control. If you spread the effect, maybe the target
will still conclude it's kids."

"Right. I'll get on it right now. Maybe I'll get
there before he tries to put a key in his lock. Call
you later."

They broke their connection, and Buzz turned
to Bonnie.

Brusquely, he said, "C'mon. We've got to go
back there as fast as we can. You know the way, so
you drive, and bring your damned glue." He shut
down his computer and propelled Bonnie toward
the door.

"Wait a minute," Bonnie said, trying to pull
her arm from Buzz's grasp. "What's this all about?
What are you going to do?"

"I'll tell you on the way."

As Bonnie drove toward the scene of the
"crime," Buzz decided it was time to impress Bonnie with the seriousness of their situation. Maintaining his calm with effort, he said, "Bonnie, I've
tried not to mention this to you before because I
didn't want to alarm you unnecessarily. But now
you've got to know the sordid truth. Skeeg isn't
just some kind of weirdo—he's a genuine socio-

path."

"Meaning what?"

"For one thing, they can be very dangerous."

"How?"

"To be specific, sociopaths are manipulative, glib, and charming. That explains why Skeeg can be so successful as a salesman, while still hiding his true character. They're like chameleons who can change from Jekyll to Hyde in an instant to suit their purposes. They're also pathological liars, and have no feelings of shame or guilt. Everything that goes wrong is always someone else's fault, which explains why he's blaming *you* for all his troubles. Worse, sociopaths can live in your neighborhood for years without anyone suspecting there's a monster living just down the street. There's more, but that should help you understand what we're dealing with here."

Bonnie drove without speaking for several miles. "I—I haven't had any experience with these kinds of people—at least, not that I'm aware of—so I'm having trouble believing Skeeg can be that ... but I'm beginning to see how horribly stupid my idea was."

"I'm sorry, but I felt I had to tell you the truth about what we're dealing with. Skeeg will stop at nothing to achieve his purpose. Believe me when I tell you he's dangerous."

"Why haven't you told me this before?" *I wonder how he knows about these kinds of things—*

*and why. That's something else I'd like to explore
while sitting by the fire, if all is not lost.*

"I already told you, I didn't want to alarm you
unnecessarily, but now that you know what he is,
you should act accordingly."

Arriving at their destination, Bonnie parked
where she had before. She turned off her lights as
Buzz instructed.

"Gimme the glue," he directed, still in no
mood to be tactful. When Bonnie complied, he left
the car, closing the door as quietly as he could. After scanning the street for pedestrians and seeing
none in sight, he crossed and headed for the front
door of the condo adjacent to Skeeg's. After
squirting glue into its lock, he repeated the procedure at the next three houses down the block, as
well as at Skeeg's neighbor in the other direction.
Then he returned to Bonnie's car and got in.

"Let's get out of here."

On the way home, conversation was sparse,
except that Buzz did make Bonnie promise not to
make any further "stupid moves." She readily
agreed; there was no doubt in her mind the anger
directed at her was deep, and that Buzz had been
hurt by her action. Her hope for a serious relationship with Buzz seemed to have evaporated with a
single thoughtless action. Stealing a glance in his
direction, she noted the signs—jutting jaw, eyes
straight ahead, scowling face.

Bonnie also fretted about Skeeg's reaction to

the gluing of his door lock, and about her ability to appear innocent if the topic came up tomorrow. If he had been in a foul mood today, what would he be like tomorrow? But mostly, she wondered if she had lost her chances with Buzz forever.

Chapter Twenty-Two

At ten-thirty the following morning, Skeeg drove into the parking garage with tires squealing. Braking hard, he turned his BMW into a parking space, lost control, and banged into the solid concrete wall in front of him.

"Sonuvabitch," he shouted, slamming his hands hard against the steering wheel. Throwing his door open, he got out to assess the damage. "Dammit," he growled, "this is all I need." The damage to the car consisted of broken headlights and a dented radiator, but the damage to his frame of mind was much worse. He was now certain that something was happening to him he couldn't control. Could this strange series of events have been a coincidence? Or was some sinister hand reaching out to frustrate his every act? No, that couldn't be. After all, ramming the car against the wall was something *he* did. He must be losing his mind. If that Nesbitt hadn't been ragging him for that damned report ...

At ten-forty, Skeeg stormed into his office and

threw his wastebasket against the wall, slamming it into a picture frame and shattering the glass.

As the shards settled to the floor, Brenda, alarmed at the unexpected outburst, leaped aside. "More problems?"

"Lemme alone," Skeeg barked. "I don't need a busybody right now. Get lost."

At eleven, Skeeg exploded into Bonnie's office. "I need you to help me finish this blasted report for Nesbitt," he blurted.

"I thought you'd already finished it." Bonnie had forgotten about the second version vanishing from Skeeg's computer.

"I *did,* but my blasted computer lost it again. And I'm late again today because of some vandalism in our neighborhood last night."

Bonnie couldn't help noticing his flushed face, the sweat sliding down his cheeks and neck, soaking into his collar. She saw the bulging veins in his neck and the heaving of his chest. *My God,* she thought. *He's hyperventilating. This is the first time I've seen him so strung out I can actually* smell *him.*

She tried to keep her voice even. "Oh?"

"Yeah. Some sonuvabitch filled our front door locks with glue, dammit. Up and down the street. Must have been those rotten neighborhood kids out on a lark looking for some kind of damage to do."

"I'm sorry to hear that." Bonnie was relieved

he thought the problem was caused by kids, and ecstatic that the caper had occupied Skeeg for yet another evening. She'd appreciated another good night's sleep, in spite of the guilt she felt about the inconvenience to Skeeg's neighbors.

She tried very hard to keep a serious expression on her face as she listened to his tale of woe. This would not be a good time to incite him further. Any further provocation might easily lead to violence.

"The neighbors and I had to get a locksmith out first thing this morning—which wasn't easy," Skeeg said. "But even *that* wasn't all." Skeeg shook his head in disbelief. "When I went to get gas, my *other* tire was flat."

"Another nail?"

"No, and that's the weirdest thing. When we finally got the garage to send a guy out to the gas station to change the tire, he said there wasn't anything *wrong* with the tire. Took 'im a long time to find out that the little gismo inside the valve stem had loosened just enough to cause a slow leak. Can you believe that? By the time I got to the gas station, the tire was *flat*."

"Did they get it fixed?"

"Yeah. All they had to do was tighten up the little gismo and fill the tire with air. Said they'd never heard of that happening before." Skeeg shook his head. "I *must* be jinxed."

"Do they know how it happened?"

"Well, it couldn't have been kids, because the valve cap was still screwed on. Could have vibrated loose, I suppose, but dammit, it shouldn't be happening to *me*."

Bonnie bent down to flick an imaginary speck from a shoe to hide her enormous relief.

"So I need your help to get caught up with that report."

Bonnie had almost forgotten about tampering with Skeeg's valve stem, and fervently hoped Buzz wouldn't find out about this second lapse in judgment. "I'll be glad to do what I can," she said. She accompanied Skeeg to his office, reviewed the partial draft, then returned to her office to add the missing sections.

Shortly thereafter, Skeeg left for lunch. Brenda wasted no time getting on the phone to the other associates, spreading the word about Skeeg's angry outburst. She remembered to include that nice Twila who worked for Mr. Nesbitt.

"Yes," she said to Twila. "He clomped in ... really late again, threw his wastebasket against the wall, and then hollered at me to go away. All I was doing was putting a memo on his desk. I'm scared, Twila. He seems to be getting more unhinged every day. I just don't know what to do to please him."

The story had spread throughout the building by the time everyone had returned from lunch. It spread to Court Nesbitt as well, who had overheard a conversation in the hallway. Returning quickly to his office, he made yet another note in the personnel file of one Bartley Skeeg.

*   *   *

During her lunch break, Bonnie managed to slip away from her colleagues to call Buzz from her cell phone. Recounting the scuttlebutt spreading throughout the company, she described Skeeg's erratic actions when entering her office. She refrained from mentioning the valve stem caper.

"Good," Buzz said. "You did the right thing by agreeing to help him."

"Thank you. But now I'm scared. Maybe we're pushing him too far."

"Not yet. Can you join me this evening? It's Friday, and you've probably got a date or something. If you're free, though, we should talk. The phone you're calling from is far from secure."

"No," Bonnie said. "I don't have a date ... at least I didn't, until just now." She might as well plant the idea that she'd welcome a real date with this man. Maybe, just maybe, all was not lost.

"Great. If you've got the courage, it's my turn to cook."

"I'm game."

"How about some Army chow?"

"Uh ..."

"Just kidding. Maybe I can scrape up a little

roadkill or something"

"*Buzz—*"

"Okay, okay. It's just that I'm sort of delight-ing in the sound of your voice. I know I shouldn't say this, but since you can't kill me over the phone, I think you're cute as hell when you're miffed."

"Oh, you *do,* do you? Wait, does that mean you're not mad at me anymore?"

"Of course not. I was for awhile, until I real-ized you're not very good at predicting conse-quences. Actually, I forgave you your dumb play as soon as I saw you wiggle your tail out of the car last night."

Bonnie's spirits soared. "Well, in *that* case, you just wait till I get my hands on you, you—"

"Ahh, music to my ears. Come when you're ready. We'll dine with candles—dress according-ly." With those words he hung up, leaving Bonnie with a dead phone in her hand.

"I think I've just been involved in a bit of fore-play," she said to the silent phone, smiling in anti-cipation of what she hoped would follow.

After the tense day, Bonnie treated herself to a leisurely bath, bubbles and all. She luxuriated in the pleasant fragrance from the rose-scented bub-ble-bath, in Fang chirping the events of his day, and in the absence of a ringing telephone. *If only Buzz were here to wash my back.*

Later, refreshed and ready to greet the world, she studied her mirrored image and pondered what to wear. "We dine with candles," Buzz had said. What did he mean by that? Never mind, she would dress provocatively. No bag-wear tonight! *Would a cocktail dress be too formal? Mmm, yes. It's a warm, pleasant fall evening in the desert, so something just a teeny bit more casual, I think.*

Rummaging through her closet, she found a soft, turquoise dress. It had a scoop neckline, and the fabric floated from the waist down. The bodice, relatively form-fitting and nip-waisted, clung closely and seductively. With strappy, high-heeled matching sandals completing the outfit, the effect was sexy and appealing, without screaming "Hey! Come seduce me!"

After one last peek into her mirror to fluff her hair, she locked the door and sauntered the short distance to her neighbor's house. She pushed the bell button and stood back a pace to give Buzz a clear picture of the woman standing before him.

"Wow!" Buzz exclaimed. "I see before me a vision of loveliness."

"Thank you, kind sir. You look surprised."

"Ah, it's just that I don't often see you dressed like a real woman." He knew immediately his words didn't convey his intended meaning. He'd put his foot in it again.

"That sounds suspiciously like a chauvinist comment ... but I'll overlook it this time." Bonnie definitely enjoyed Buzz's discomfort. "You're looking kind of cool, yourself. That blue blazer over the white outfit is rather dashing."

"Gee, thanks."

"Aren't you going to invite me in?"

"Oh, sure. Sorry." He was suddenly embarrassed that they were still standing in the doorway. "I'm so dazzled, I'm forgetting my manners. Please come in and make yourself at home. How about a dollop of scotch to get things started?"

"You tryin' to get me tiddly?"

"Only a little. David and I need to talk to you about something, and half-tiddly will be just about right."

"I don't think I like the sound of that. What's it all about?"

"Let's wait until we're all on line together, okay?" He poured scotch on the rocks, they clinked glasses, and sipped.

"Y'know," Bonnie said, "I really do like your expensive taste in liquor. This is a fine scotch."

"I have a friend who says, 'If it's worth doing at all, it's worth doing to excess.' That sort of says it all. If you'll excuse me, I need to put the salad on the table. We're using the dining room tonight."

"Can I help?"

"Just find an empty seat at the table and I'll be there in twenty-seven milliseconds."

Bonnie wandered into the dining room and immediately noticed the fine antique table for the first time. Though it was covered by a linen tablecloth, she could tell the legs had been individually handcrafted.

"How old is this table?" she said, directing the question toward the kitchen.

"It was handed down from my grandfather, so it must be close to a hundred years old, at least. As you can see, it's not a really big table ... just the right size for a bachelor like me."

Bonnie fantasized a life with Buzz where she could sit with him at this table every day of their lives. "It's lovely." Two black candles burned in silver candlestick holders at opposite ends of a floral centerpiece of gardenias. She bent over and sniffed, breathing in their heavenly fragrance.

Buzz entered with a salad plate in each hand, placing them at opposite ends of the table. The salad—cold cooked shrimp arrayed on a bed of lettuce—was accompanied by a small container of cocktail sauce.

"It's been a long time since I've had shrimp salad, and never as nicely presented as this. Is this catered?"

"You wound me, madam. *Nothing* in this house is catered ... well, except for an occasional pizza."

"It's just that it looks so ... so professionally prepared."

"Gee, thanks a *lot*. Talk about chauvinistic comments—women think guys can't do anything in the kitchen for themselves. But I'll have you know, dear lady, that I also heat a mean hot dog.

Not to mention other things."

"I'll bet you do. Seriously, where'd you learn to cook?"

"It's a long story, but I'd like to save it for a wintry evening around a fire, if you don't mind."

Bonnie immediately saw the scene on the wide screen of her imagination. Somewhere in Sedona, a roaring fire crackled in the fireplace, snow fell outside, as the two of them huddled lovingly, staring at the blaze. She longed to turn the fantasy into reality, and wished for the magic that might bring it about.

The main course, proudly served by Buzz, was an authentic Hungarian chicken paprikas, accompanied by equally authentic cabbage and dumplings.

"Holy Maloney, that smells good," Bonnie commented. "I've been salivating ever since I walked in. How in the world did you learn to make it?" A man might learn to prepare steak and potatoes, but this—this was gourmet food. When she tasted it, her eyes widened. "This is terrific chicken. Why, it just melts in your mouth!" She lifted her glass and presented a toast. "To the most surprising man I've ever met."

Buzz beamed with pleasure.

During dinner, they reviewed the events of the day, especially those relating to Skeeg's deteriorating self-control.

Buzz agreed Skeeg was nearing the edge. "It's

time to put the finishing touches on our little project, so have another sip of wine. You need to be a
little mellow for what we've planned."

"And what *do* you have planned?

"As soon as we get on line with David, all will
be revealed." he said, twirling an imaginary Snide-
ly Whiplash moustache.

Chapter Twenty-Three

"I agree," David said. "We'd better drive toward a conclusion now—before the target goes totally over the edge—or zeros in on Bonnie."

Bonnie and Buzz nodded as David spoke over the encrypted video line.

"Bonnie, has Skeeg done anything to you at all this week?" David asked.

"No, he hasn't. As far as we know, he hasn't even parked outside the house. Whatever you're doing has worked."

"I'm happy for that."

"But I'm afraid. He's starting to throw things at the office," a frowning Bonnie said.

"Understandable," David said. "It won't go on much longer."

"Let's review the mission and ground rules before we talk about the plan." This from Buzz. "The mission is to cause Skeeg to stop stalking Bonnie, once and for all. We want to do this in a way that won't cause physical damage to anyone involved, but will prevent Skeeg from discovering who's behind his discomfort. Okay so far?" Seeing nods from both Bonnie and David, he continued. "David, you wanna tell her what we have in mind?"

"Right. Here's the theory. We've been keeping Skeeg too busy to bother you this week, which was the plan. But if we're going to put him out of action, we need to give him time to pester you so we can catch him in the act."

"In other words," Bonnie said, "you want to use me for bait."

David smiled. "I think she's onto us. Yeah. Something like that."

"And just what do you propose?"

"By leaving him alone to carry out the next items on his list. With any luck, he'll be frustrated and angry enough to skip some of the items and get down to the serious stuff."

"Such as?" Bonnie wasn't at all sure she was going to like the answer to this question.

"Such as breaking into your house again."

"*Wait* a minute," Bonnie said, standing and shaking her head. "I don't like the idea of his tearing up my house and maybe causing a lot of expensive damage that—"

"Hold on," David interrupted. "That's not the way it will work."

"Well, how *will* it work?"

"By the time he gets into your house, both you and Buzz will be there to put him away."

"Put him away?"

"Subdue him."

"Look!" Bonnie said, forcefully. "I know *you* guys know what you're talking about, but I'm not following your code here. How about laying it out in plain English?"

"Okay," David said. "Here's what we envision. First, we lay off Skeeg to give him time to think about his next move. That shouldn't take more than a couple of days. Between now and then, you stay out of your house and out of harm's way."

"Exactly where do you expect me to stay?"

"With Ram ... er, Buzz."

"You expect me to stay *here?*"

"Please, let me finish. You stay with Buzz because that will accomplish several things. First, it will keep you out of danger. Second, you'll both be close by and ready for action when he shows up. Third, with the alarms Buzz has rigged, you'll know when he arrives to do his dirty work."

Bonnie thought about the implications of David's speech. It wasn't that she minded staying with Buzz, but what about the neighbors? What would they think when they saw her coming and going from his house during the day?

Buzz reached out and stroked her arm. "You're worried about what the neighbors might think, is that it?"

"How did you—yes, that's one of the things."

"Look, Bonnie. You're being stalked by a very dangerous man, and you're adamant about not going to the police for what you consider to be good reasons. We can respect that. So the neighbors' feelings are far, far less important than keeping you out of danger. Besides ... I'd kinda like having you around."

"You would?"

"As the song says," he added, "I've grown accustomed to your face."

Bonnie's eyes widened. Was this a proposal? No, couldn't be. That wouldn't be consistent with his character. What, then? An invitation to "shack up" for a couple of nights? No, that wasn't consistent, either.

"This house has three bedrooms."

Bonnie grimaced. *He actually does read minds.*

"There's one more thing," David said. "You'll have to take some time off from work. Tell them you've got to spend a day or two with one of your other clients. Can you handle that?"

"No problem. It's time I had a meeting with a California client about the next phase of their project. That's something I have to do face-to-face. Felina and Amalina are managing most of the office work on the Marsden project. I'll just tell them I'll be in Los Angeles for a couple days."

"Make sure they spread the word so Skeeg knows your house will be empty."

"That'll be the easiest part. I'll just leave a message for him with Brenda. Then everyone will know."

"Fine. Buzz, we've got a full weekend ahead of us. Maybe we'd better keep Skeeg busy until Monday."

"Don't think we'll need to. From Bonnie's description, he's so strung out he's likely to take the weekend off himself."

"Okay, but stay vigilant. 'Bye for now." They broke the connection.

"Well," Buzz asked, "what do you think?"

"Frankly, I'm not sure. I need to mull it over."

"May I make a suggestion?"

"Of course."

"I propose we return to the dining room for dessert and coffee. We can talk there."

"Good idea."

Dessert turned out to be a silver plate filled with lusciously rich Godiva chocolates arrayed on a linen doily. The coffee was excellent, the brandy divine. As they reviewed their discussion with David, Bonnie began formulating a list of things she would need to bring over from her house. It was as though she were moving in—the idea excited her, making her feel tingly all over.

As the evening progressed, the discussion ranged far and wide, and the conversation edged closer and closer toward their inner souls.

"There's something I've been meaning to ... to ask you," Bonnie began, unsure about how to address the issue uppermost in her heart. The dollop of brandy, however, gave her the courage to attack the issue head-on.

"What? I've already told you everything there is to know about me."

"Not quite," she said, softly. Reaching out a hand and placing it lightly on Buzz's fingers, she let the silence hang in the air.

Sensing something significant in the offing, Buzz sat very still, waiting patiently.

Finally, Bonnie spoke. "I'm not sure how to say this, so please forgive me if I say it badly."

Buzz nodded, but just barely, not wanting to interrupt.

"We had a rather rocky beginning, what with my threatening to kill you and all, but as time passed I think we've become pretty good friends."

Another nod.

"We've even shared some rather passionate kisses ... kisses I've enjoyed very much, by the way. But ... but ... every time I think the kisses might lead to something more, you pull back and run away. So, I'd like to ask you straight out ... what is there about me you don't like? Do I do something that repels you? I'd really like to know." Bonnie breathed a sigh of relief. "There. I said it."

Buzz was stunned. He'd had no idea she was blaming herself for the tension between them. "Oh, Bonnie. I'm so sorry," he began, clasping her hand with both of his own. "I'm really sorry. I know exactly what you're referring to, but you're wrong, so very wrong for blaming yourself. I ... I haven't been able to talk about it until now, but maybe it's time I finally tried. Let me begin by asking *your* forgiveness in case I say *this* badly."

Bonnie nodded in silence, eager to learn what Buzz was about to tell her.

"You're right, you know. I *do* pull back and run away, as you put it, but believe me when I tell you it has nothing whatever to do with *you*. Uh ... what I mean is, there is nothing whatsoever *wrong* with you. Actually, I find myself enjoying everything about you. In fact, I find you more attractive than any other woman I've known."

"Then—?"

Buzz held up a hand to stop her from continuing.

"Now I've started, you'd better let me tell it my way. I've never spoken of this to anyone, not even to myself. So my story might not be entirely coherent." Buzz paused for another sip of brandy, and to collect his thoughts.

"It's like this. After a rocky start, my father became a very successful stockbroker. He managed his own office employing several brokers, knew a lot of influential people, and managed to become pretty well off. He also did a lot of charity things. And I admired him—a lot. There wasn't *anything* I wouldn't do to try to please him."

"Then one day he came to me and told me he had just the right woman for me, and extolled the

virtues of a person he made sound like the perfect
mate. I wasn't too keen on his choosing someone
for me. Hey, that practice, after all, went out of
style some time ago. Like every young person, I
was bent on marrying someone I loved, rather
than someone chosen for me by my father. So I
bristled when he brought it up." He looked down
at the snifter in his hand, staring at the golden liquid. He couldn't yet look directly at Bonnie as he
spoke.

"My father assured me he wasn't trying to
pressure me into a marriage that didn't please me.
It was just that he was totally convinced this was a
woman I had to meet and get to know. So I agreed
to do at least that.

"He arranged a meeting, and we were introduced. She turned out to be everything my father
promised—attractive, well-mannered, polite, and
so on. But there were some things that she wasn't.
For one thing, she wasn't any fun. At *all*. Everything she did or said was calculated to impress her
friends, or her father's business contacts. Later, I
realized my father's hidden agenda was to have me
seen with her at important functions—important
to my father, that is. At that point I felt rather
ashamed, and used, by a father I'd idolized."

Bonnie lifted his hand and squeezed her understanding.

Buzz smiled, and continued, "For another
thing, she wasn't at all willing to let me be me.

From the moment we met, she tried to dominate my life with a social calendar organized entirely without my knowledge or consent. She'd tell me where we were going, what I should wear, what and what not to say. You can't imagine how stifling it was—and boring. Absolutely nothing about that social calendar had anything to do with me or my interests.

"The worst part was that, whenever I tried to dance close to her, or tried to kiss her, she made me feel like a sexual predator. She had an endless supply of put-downs. During those rare kisses when she felt me getting aroused, she would push me away and stamp around the room in an angry fit. She'd shout every insult she could think of, and then some. She made me feel like a depraved animal, interested only in ravishing her precious body.

"It wasn't until much later I learned the history behind that abnormal behavior. Seems her father had been treated to the same anti-male environment. When he decided he'd had enough, he simply packed his things and left—for good. The mother was totally humiliated by her husband's rejection of her, so much so that she nurtured a hatred for men that lasted the rest of her life.

"And all that hatred rubbed off on her daughter. I often wonder why I put up with the degradation for as long as I did ... and I've flogged myself a thousand times for my weakness. But I did it for my father. He'd told me he wouldn't force me into a marriage with someone of his choosing, and that made it easier for me to stay with it, at least for a while.

"Finally, I'd had enough. I simply stopped showing up at the functions she'd scheduled. When I heard she was furious at my absence, I rejoiced. Soon after that, I joined the Army and didn't have to feel guilty about standing her up any more."

Bonnie remained silent, sensing something still unsaid.

"This is the hard part. That all happened when I was at a pretty impressionable age, you see, and it wasn't until later I finally understood my self-confidence with women had been damaged more than I realized. Since then, I've dated some—but not much. I've even met some women who were a lot of fun to be with. But I've never been able to ... to get close to them. I've tried, but as soon as I get close enough to become even slightly aroused, the hurt from the vicious words of that snotty-assed woman come flooding back. I know it doesn't make sense, and I know I should have gotten over it by now, but it's still there. Believe me, it has *nothing* to do with you." Buzz grasped Bonnie's hand tightly in both of his.

"As a matter of fact, for some time now I've been longing to be able to take you in my arms and shower your beautiful body with kisses. But every time I try ...."

Bonnie sat perfectly still, a single tear of compassion twinkling on her cheek.

"Well, that's the story. Pretty silly, isn't it?"

"You poor man." There was nothing Bonnie wanted more at that moment than to take him in her arms and squeeze the hurt out of him, forever. "There's nothing silly about it, and it makes me feel special that you were able to tell me. All this time I've been wondering what I was doing that bugged you."

"The answer is nothing, absolutely nothing— except that you can't seem to follow orders."

Bonnie let the dig at her gluing caper pass. "I think I understand the discomfort you must feel, but please don't give up. Not all women are alike, you know."

"I'm sure that must be true. But knowing it, and acting on it, aren't quite the same."

"If you'll give me a chance, I'd like to try to do something about the situation." Bonnie smiled, hoping she wasn't being too forward.

Buzz smiled in return. "You wanna be my *romance* counselor?"

"You can put it that way, if you want."

Buzz thought for a moment, then said, "Yes, I think that would be very nice. What do we do first?"

"Well ... I still have a goodly supply of unused kisses. Would you think it too forward of me if I offered up a couple right now?"

They both stood, smiling, and faced each other. Their hands met, and they looked deeply and solemnly into each other's eyes.

Buzz reached up to brush the tear from her damp cheek. "I'm ready for my first counseling session."

"Then we'll begin right now." Exhilarated at the position she had talked herself into, Bonnie decided to take command of the situation. "Right now I'm going to kiss you, and I don't want you even to *think* about pulling away. Before I do, though, I want to make it clear ... absolutely clear that I *like* being touched ... and held ... and kissed ... and everything." With that, she reached up and pulled his head to hers, their lips meeting with mutual desire. Bonnie felt the electricity all over again, all the way to her toes, as a warm, moist feeling of expectation spread throughout her soul.

The kiss lasted a long, long time. When at last their lips parted, Bonnie bit him gently on the nose, and kissed him again.

"Y'know," she said, "you don't kiss like a virgin."

Another kiss.

"Whoever said I was a virgin is a liar. I lost that title long before the Ice Dragon came along."

More kisses—and entwining of tongues.

"I thought you said you couldn't get close enough to women to have sex."

More kisses, interspersed with biting of lips.

"That problem developed long after I lost my virginity."

A blizzard of butterfly kisses, punctuated by more tongue dancing.

"You've been growing on me ever since you stopped promising to kill me. I truly care about you, Bonnie."

"Then why—"

"Because I didn't want to scare you away thinking I was a sex-crazed maniac."

Bonnie looked at the unruly curl bobbling on Buzz's forehead. "I think I understand, finally." She placed his hand on her bosom and squeezed gently.

"Y'know, I think you must have the most perfect breasts in the entire world," Buzz whispered.

"How would *you* know? You've never even *looked* at them."

"You wound me, madam. Who was it repaired your broken strap after you nearly killed that poor Skeeg guy? You think I was doing that with my eyes closed?"

"Poor man, my ass. Wait a minute ... you were ogling my breasts?"

"Drinking them in, good lady. Ogling to the very hilt. And if I weren't so well-bred I'd drag you to the bedroom by the hair and ravish your gorgeous body this very instant."

"You *would?*" Bonnie's breath came faster

and her heart began to pound.

"I definitely would. But you might batter me all over the room and—"

"In my condition, sir, I believe my resistance to such an outrageous attack would be token, at best." She pressed her body tighter against his. "And if I'm not mistaken, I believe your weapon is ready to be unsheathed."

Without loosening their hold on one another, they kissed and shuffled, shuffled and kissed, all the way to the bedroom.

Chapter Twenty-Four

During the pillow-talk following a most glorious love-symphony exceeding Bonnie's wildest imaginings, their fingers traced lazy circles around each other's chests and ears as they made weekend plans. Each was eager to spend as much time together as the world allowed.

"Angela's coming over tomorrow morning for our bi-weekly workout at ten ... you can send Blackie over to flirt with us if you want," Bonnie said.

"Promise not to hose him out of the sky?"

"I wouldn't dream of it. Blackie's a lot more polite than Heli ever was."

"In that case, I'll keep him in a high state of readiness."

"What'll we do after that?"

"Hey, I know. The neighborhood kids are coming over at three. How about coming over to help out?"

"That'd be fun. But what could I do?"

"Don't worry," Buzz said. "They'll keep you

plenty busy. And after we get rid of the urchins, I'll make some dinner and we can sit around a roaring fire."

"A fire in the middle of fall? Are you *nuts?*"

"I just happen to have a video of a nice crackling fire—generates no heat at all. We'll have to make our own."

"You're *weird,* but I like it. We can roast virtual marshmallows."

"Who you calling weird?" Buzz rolled over onto Bonnie and kissed her gruffly. "Take that, you hussy."

"Did I mention you're weird? And what's that thing poking me in the belly? Seems like everybody wants to get into the act."

"Excellent idea. Let's put on an act it can get into."

Which they did. Again.

"*Ayeee!*" Bonnie suddenly shrieked, jumping from the bed and grabbing for her clothing.

"What's wrong?" Buzz sat up, alarmed at her sudden outburst.

"*Fang!* I've forgotten all about *Fang.*" She gathered her clothing as quickly as her fumbling fingers would allow.

"You leap out of a passionate embrace for a *bird?* Guess I know where *I* stand. Hey, don't you have a bird feeder on the cage? And a water dish?"

Bonnie stopped, her hand over her mouth. "Of *course* I do, and I filled them before coming

over here, come to think of it." Her face reddened
with embarrassment.

"Then get back in bed. There's something I
want to show you."

She dropped her clothing and did as she was
told.

*   *   *

Sweat dripping from their bodies after a gruel-
ing workout—kick-boxing, step-dancing, and just
plain calisthenics—Bonnie and Angela dragged
themselves to the house. Taking turns at shower-
ing, they chatted as they took their time nailing
themselves into presentable condition.

"Bonnie, my friend, you were *brutal* this
morning," Angela said. "Where did you get all that
energy?"

"I cannot tell a lie. I spent the night with
Buzz."

"You *did?* Wow!   How did you manage to
make that happen?"

"Simple. I got a little bit mellow on the
brandy, and then just asked him point-blank why
he didn't find me attractive."

"You're kidding!"

"No. That's pretty much the way it happened."

"Amazing. So what was there about you he
didn't find attractive?"

"*Nothing*. Nothing at all ... and that's the delicious part of it. It was all in his head."

"I don't get it."

"He kept pulling away because of a bad experience he had years ago with a woman who ought to be strung up. He doesn't have any trouble at all in the love-making department. He just wasn't able to make sexual advances, because it brought back memories of the crazy woman he calls the 'Ice Dragon.' But I helped him to finally get over that problem."

"How'd you manage to do that?"

"One step at a time, Angela, one step at a time. When he broke through the hang-up, he at last confessed that he cares about me. He's really a very passionate lover."

"I say again, wow! Was the 'L' word mentioned?"

"Not yet. We need more time—"

"Don't let him get away."

*   *   *

By the time Bonnie came within ten feet of Buzz's basement, she could hear shouts and laughter from the kids gathered there to work on their model airplane projects. When she entered, it was as though she were invisible; everyone was far too busy to notice her. But what she saw made her smile.

There were four kids present, including the

Buzz "kid." Dressed in what she hoped were their grungiest clothes, they were totally absorbed. The three *actual* kids must have ranged in age from seven to nine, Bonnie guessed; the Buzz "kid" was, of course, somewhat older.

Finally noticing her presence, Buzz shouted to the busy workers.

"Hey guys, I want you to meet my friend, Bonnie. She's going to help us out today. Bonnie, meet Billy, Ron, and Clarissa!

"Hi, everybody! I'm very happy to meet you all."

Introductions out of the way, Buzz explained the projects in progress. He then invited the budding "aeronautical engineers" to show Bonnie their almost-completed model airplanes, which each did with great enthusiasm. They were so proud of their accomplishments, their tongues had trouble keeping up with their thoughts.

"Mine's gonna fly the highest ..." (Billy.)

"Mine's gonna fly the fastest ..." (Ron.)

"Mine'll beat theirs. And it's the prettiest, too." (Clarissa.)

Milliseconds later, they were all back, hard at work carving, cutting, pasting, gluing. The smell of airplane glue, and the chatter of little-people talk, filled the basement. Buzz offered tactful guidance when needed, and Bonnie kept busy locating supplies, mopping up occasional spills, and de-cluttering the work areas enough to prevent tools and supplies from being totally swallowed by the debris.

She worked with a perpetual smile, for more than one reason. She genuinely enjoyed her role in this delightful enterprise, and hoped it would be the first of many such occasions. But her biggest joy came from watching Buzz. She could tell he genuinely liked these kids. His gentleness, his patience, his firmness when required, painted a promising picture in her mind. *It's really true,* she declared silently—*there really isn't anything this man can't do! No wonder the neighbors don't complain about the occasional noise.* Angela was right—this was not a man to let get away. This was the man for *her.*

"Are you in love with Mr. Toolen?" Bonnie was torn from her reverie by the unexpected question from Clarissa, who couldn't have been older than eight.

"Don't be so *nosy,*" Ron offered.

"Yeah," Billy added. "Mind your own beeswax."

Clarissa, however, was not easily dissuaded. Besides, boys were easy to tune out. "Well, *are* you?" she persisted.

Bonnie's face reddened, and Buzz thought she looked especially beautiful when she blushed.

"Uhh … well … I'm very fond of Mr. Toolen and—"

"Are you gonna *marry* him?" Clarissa again.

At that, Buzz stepped in.

"Okay, I think that's enough. It isn't polite to ask such personal questions, you know."

At which point Clarissa turned her curiosity in *his* direction. "Well, do *you* love *her?*"

"Aw, knock off the mushy stuff, already," Ron said. "Let's get back to work."

"Why do girls always have to be so *icky?*" Billy bopped Ron on the shoulder with a fist. "See? I told you we never shoulda let her in."

"It's okay, guys. Take it easy." Buzz locked eyes with Bonnie. "All you need to know is that I am very fond of this lady."

Total silence from the gallery.

On a sudden whim, he added, "And I'm even willing to prove it." Striding the few steps to Bonnie, he took her in his arms, leaned her backward with a masterful air of formality, and kissed her soundly.

A noisy chorus of critical comment arose from the boys, accompanied by applause from Clarissa.

"*Eeewww.*"

"*Gross!*"

"*Yay!*"

Clearly, Buzz's action had received mixed reviews. He would have to re-build his reputation with the boys, kissing definitely not being included in a small boy's definition of "manly." As for Clarissa, he was certain she could hardly wait to tell everyone she knew what she *saw* Mr. Toolen *doing* in his basement.

But Clarissa wasn't through pestering Bonnie. "Are you gonna get married?"

"Uhh, some day I hope to get married. Don't you?"

A slick response, Buzz thought. *Noncommittal, yet responsive to the question. She'd have done well in law school.*

"I mean to *him*," Clarissa added, pointing a glue-encrusted finger toward Buzz.

"Well," Bonnie said, "That's a big secret. Tell you what. As soon as the secret can be told, how about if we promise that you will be the first to know?"

That hint of conspiracy seemed to satisfy Clarissa's curiosity, at least for the moment. Buzz breathed a sigh of relief. The boys, who were already back at work on their projects, couldn't have cared less.

*   *   *

Later that evening, Buzz called David on the encrypted line.

"I know I said we didn't need to, but now I think we need to keep Skeeg too busy to harass Bonnie over the week-end. I'm a little worried he might take action before we're ready. You okay with that?"

"I'm already on it. I think he'll be kept busy

answering his phone. Several telemarketers some-how got his number on their hot lists. Also, if he checks his email, he'll find a bundle waiting to be sorted through. If he can get through the virus, that is."

"How'd that happen?"

"How would I know?" An angelic expression of innocence spread across David's face.

"Right. I think it's gonna hit the fan on Mon-day. As we planned, Bonnie's gonna have her as-sociates pass the word that she's left town to spend some time with another client."

"Perfect. That'll be the time for selected exec-utives to find a copy of the 'Bitch' file on their ma-chines. Think I ought to send it along to the police there as well?"

"Uh, no. It's a long shot, but the cops might take action on it before Skeeg goes into his act."

Monday morning, Bonnie called her primary associate, Felina Zhang.

"I'm leaving for the West Coast in a few min-utes, Felina. Got a call from our project manager at Honda. Wants me to spend a day with him working out a few bugs. I should be back by noon Tuesday."

"Lucky you."

"Yeah. Please be sure to call Brenda as soon as possible and ask her to tell Skeeg I'll be out of town for the entire day tomorrow."

"Sure. Anything else?"

"Nope. Just make sure Brenda gets the message."

That evening after dark, a caravan of two sneaky people crept across the lawns toward Buzz's house. He carried a covered birdcage in one hand, a suitcase in the other. Bonnie toted her make-up case in one hand and a garment bag over a shoulder with the other. Hoping for invisibility during the migration from her house to his, they'd each dressed for the short trek in dark "skulking clothes."

"I feel like a burglar escaping from the scene of the crime," Bonnie whispered.

"And I feel like I've just kidnapped the only eye-witness to a brutal murder." He held up the birdcage to dramatize his point. What he didn't say is he felt like someone who had just kidnapped his intended from the clutches of an evil landlord.

After settling in and allowing Bonnie unpacking time, he appeared at the bedroom door with a scotch-on-the-rocks in each hand. Clinking the glasses, he said, "Here. They've already been pre-clinked by an expert."

"Do I detect the presence of the resident debaucher?" she asked, taking the proffered glass.

"You do indeed, madam, and I will foreclose on your delinquent mortgage unless you allow me to have my way with you." He stroked an imaginary mustache with a flourish.

"Oh, sir, sir," pleaded Bonnie, now on her

knees with outstretched arms. "Please do not send me into the streets without my beloved mortgage. I promise to do your every bidding."

"In that case," Buzz said, waggling an imaginary cigar, "I bid three spades."

Bonnie stood and shook her head. "You *are* weird, you know that?" Accompanying her words with a smile and shake of the head, Bonnie was learning that silly banter was one of his favorite preliminaries to foreplay. She liked that.

*   *   *

Meanwhile, Bartley Skeeg fumed at being compelled to work Sunday evening to catch up on Bonnie's latest report. He had never had to do that before, and it was humiliating. That was bad enough, but his intention had been interrupted when he discovered a virus on his computer. It wasn't a virus that scrambled everything on the screen, or erased files, but it was nerve-wracking nonetheless. Every time he hit a key on his keyboard, it typed five copies of a *different* letter. When he tried to type "now," what showed on his screen was "rrrrruuuuuttttt." Completely frustrated, he finally shut off the machine and headed for home.

He dropped into a chair with a stiff drink in one hand; with the other he leafed through the latest issue of the company magazine.

"Sonuvabitch," he stormed. There, on the cen-
terfold, was a feature article describing Bonnie and
her project. A double-page spread, no less! In
glowing terms, the article described the latest results of the sales program tryouts. Moreover, it
went into detail about the favorable implications
for improved sales at Marsden Manufacturing's
overseas markets. Nowhere did it mention Bartley
Skeeg.

"This is too much," he wailed. "They make her
sound like some kind of Wonder Woman, or something, come down from above to save all the god-
damned sinners!" The more he read, the more he
growled and groaned. The more he fumed, the
more he drank, and the more he drank, the more
his mood changed from foul to charcoal black.

"That bitch's been tryin'a show me up ever
since I got stuck into this job. If it hadn't been for
all the shitty things happening this week, I'd have
taken care of her long ago." Flinging the offending
magazine toward the far end of the room, he exclaimed, "Well, this is *it!* She's gotten away with it
long enough." With that, he gulped the remains of
his drink and stormed toward the carport.

Chapter Twenty-Five

Skeeg failed to carry out his mission that night, however, as he was stopped by a patrol car for weaving from one side of his lane to the other. After pulling over and stopping in response to the flashing lights and growling siren, he was ordered to step out of his car by the biggest police officer he'd ever seen. Noting the difficulty with which Skeeg managed to open the door and untangle his feet on their way to the ground, the officer asked him to walk a straight line. When Skeeg stumbled, he was asked to close his eyes and touch his nose. He missed by a mile.

"Wait," Skeeg said, his voice slurred. "I c'n do that," and tried again. He touched his ear.

"I think you'd better blow into this tube," the officer said, handing Skeeg the plastic mouthpiece of a Breathalyzer. Skeeg did as he was told, but even in his state, he knew he'd failed when the officer cited him for DUI.

"*Now* can I go?" Skeeg asked, every fiber of his body screaming at him to punch out this police officer who dared interfere with his plans.

"Yes, sir. As soon as you call someone to take you home."

"It's Sunday *night,* dammit! Who the hell am I gonna call?"

"A wife, a friend, a taxi. If you can't find someone to drive you home, I'm afraid I'll have to take you to the station to sleep it off."

Skeeg opted for the taxi, which arrived thirty minutes later.

*   *   *

"Oh, you're *here,*" said Brenda, when Skeeg finally showed up for work at nine-thirty the next morning.

"Where the hell *else* would I be?" Skeeg snapped. He really was getting tired of her stating the obvious. Besides, his head hurt.

"I've a message for you. Bonnie had to go to the West Coast to work with another client today."

"She'll be gone all day?"

"That's what Felina said. She's supposed to be back by noon tomorrow."

"Good."

"Good?"

"Uhh, good that you gave me the message. Now leave me alone so I can get some work done." He closed his door.

Skeeg reached under his desk pad for his hard

copy of the "Bitch" file and studied the list of entries, looking for just the right action to pursue. *To hell with it,* he thought. *I've been pussy-footing long enough. Time to get serious.*

His eyes dropped to the bottom of the list, where he found the item he sought. He poked a finger at the page. "That's *it*. That'll get 'er attention."

"Brenda," he said as he passed her desk, "I'll be in a meeting over at the admin building for a couple of hours, but don't tell anyone where I've gone." He left the building with a determined step, still hung over, but with spirits much improved.

Chapter Twenty-Six

At around 11:00 that morning, Skeeg parked his black BMW around the corner from Bonnie's residence, his boyhood stalking experience having taught him the value of a low profile. Turning off the ignition, he slowly scanned the area without appearing to do so. No one was in sight—the worker bees were long since in their cubbies, the kiddie bees would be in school, and the gardener bees weren't likely to pay attention to a man dressed like themselves. *Perfect. In my blue coveralls,* he told himself, *I'll be invisible.*

Having satisfied himself he could work unobserved, he pulled on a pair of surgical gloves, picked up the small metal toolbox from the seat next to him, and stepped out of the car.

Striding toward Bonnie's home, Skeeg looked forward to his planned devastation. With the bitch unexpectedly out of town, this was the perfect opportunity to get even. With every step, he reflected on the pain he'd suffered at Bonnie's hands: The humiliation at the Fall Ball, the total destruction of his credibility at the meeting in the Board Room, her rejection of him as a boyfriend, and her flipping him onto the ground with a slick move. He replayed the degradation over and over. Then, as he walked toward the back, where the phone line entered the house, he paused. *Naw,* he thought, *why bother? There's nobody home.*

Ignoring the phone line, he crossed the small patio to the back door, where he was met by two depressing surprises. First, these weren't anything like the cheap locks he'd faced during his first clandestine visit. Now, there was a heavy-duty lock. Not only that, there was a shiny new high-quality deadbolt mounted a foot above the door lock.

"Shit!" he hissed. *Now what?* Opening his small toolbox, he removed the battery-operated lock pick he'd owned for years. *I haven't used this since the time we broke into the gimp's place and stole the old guy's crutch. Good thing I put in new batteries this morning.* Kneeling to insert the thin blued-steel pick into the lock core, he pulled the trigger, causing the pick to vibrate the pins inside. Simultaneously applying gentle pressure with the turning tool, he felt the core turn less than a minute later. The lock was open. *Gotcha!*

Damned if I'm gonna be subtle this *time.* Standing with his back to the door, he rammed an elbow through the glass pane nearest the doorknob. The glass shattered. As he reached through the jagged edges to unlock the deadbolt from the inside, he slashed his forearm. *Damn!* He pulled back a little, straightening his arm, and a trickle of blood made its way down his wrist to his fingers.

*   *   *

"Drat," Buzz said, pawing through the contents of his refrigerator.

"What's wrong?" Bonnie asked. Having showered and dressed after a leisurely love-making session, they were famished and ready for breakfast ... or brunch. *Anything* edible.

"I'm out of milk. I wanted to make us some French toast."

"I've got some," she said. "I'll run home and get it. It'll only take a sec."

"What if Skeeg shows up while you're there?"

"The alarm will go off here and we'll execute the plan."

"Okay, but take your panic button along, just in case."

"Right. Be right back." She sprinted to her front door just a few yards away, slid her key into the lock, and opened the door. As she stepped inside she heard the sound of glass breaking at the back of the house. Suddenly alarmed, her brain screamed, *Somebody's breaking in! Why didn't the alarm go off? Oh, my God! What do I do* now?

Leaving the front door open, and with heart

pounding, she reached for the panic button in her shirt pocket and held the button down.

*   *   *

When the alarm sounded throughout his house, Buzz raced to turn it off, hurried to the yard, and got Blackie airborne as quickly as he could. He was certain he'd have a little time; it would take Skeeg a few minutes to get through the new door locks he'd installed. Working as quickly as he could, he energized Blackie's camera and re-corder, started the quiet motor, and backed away to allow it a moment to warm up. As he did so, he reached for his cell phone and called 911.

*   *   *

"Crap!" Rolling up the sleeve of his jumpsuit, Skeeg decided he had to deal with the bleeding from the glass cut. But when he reached through the broken glass to turn the doorknob and open the door, he cut his arm again. His hand, now slip-pery with his blood, took several more seconds to turn the knob and open the door.

Closing the door behind him with a foot, he immediately headed for the bathroom, where he expected to find bandages and a roll of adhesive. But before he could crunch his way through the kitchen, he thought he heard a sound from the front of the house.

Skeeg stood still and listened. Hearing nothing, he crept silently toward the block of kitchen knives sitting next to the sink. Slowly sliding one from its wooden sheath, he moved toward the hallway.

"Bart, is that you?" Bonnie shouted. "You might as well come on out where I can see you."

Sonuvabitch! The bitch is back. Quickly returning to the back door, he opened it and then slammed it shut, hoping she would think he'd gone. He tiptoed back to the hallway.

Bonnie stood and listened. When she heard nothing, she began to creep slowly toward the kitchen.

"Are you there?" she called again. Again hearing nothing, she continued moving forward. Her heart pounded and her breathing grew rapid. When she saw the closed kitchen door and the broken glass, she unconsciously moved to find something with which to pick up the shards. Only then did she notice the trail of blood leading from the door to the counter.

Before she could scream, she was grabbed roughly from behind. A strong arm circled her waist and pulled her tight against the assailant she thought had gone. A moment later she felt the sharp blade of a knife against her throat.

"Don't move, bitch," Skeeg snarled, "or you'll cut your own damned throat."

Bonnie stopped struggling and froze. "Wh ... What do you want?" she managed to ask.

Skeeg, firmly in control behind her, sneered. "I want you to get the hell out of my life. I'm tired of your put-downs ... I'm tired of your humiliating me in public ... and I'm sure as hell tired of your uppity attitude."

"Uh ... all right. Put the knife down and we can talk about it."

"Oh, sure," he sneered. "You'd like that, wouldn't you?

"I promise I won't hurt you."

Skeeg laughed. "That's rich, that is. I've got you where I can do anything I want with you, and *you* promise not to hurt *me*. Isn't that *sweet*." With that, he squeezed her so hard she found it hard to breathe.

"Hey, Skeegy-boy," Buzz shouted from the yard. "You might as well come on out."

"Who the hell is that?" Skeeg demanded, alarmed at the presence of an unexpected "intruder."

"He's ... he's my boyfriend," Bonnie said.

"The hell he is." Tightening his hold, he began shuffling Bonnie toward the back door, broken glass crunching under their feet. "Open the damned door," he commanded her.

"I can't move," she said.

"Don't try anything funny." He loosened his grip just enough to allow her to reach the door.

She pulled the door open by its blood-stained knob.

"Don't do anything crazy," Skeeg hollered, "or I'll slice this bitch like a salami." He inched Bonnie through the door and onto the patio.

With chills running up his spine at Bonnie's predicament, Buzz stood twenty feet beyond the edge of the patio. Holding the control panel in his hand, he maneuvered Blackie to hover almost motionlessly above.

"What the hell you think you're gonna do with that stupid toy?" Skeeg kept pushing Bonnie across the small patio, planning to let her go with a sudden shove and run to his car for a quick getaway.

"You might as well smile when you say that, asshole. You're on candid camera." Buzz reached into his pocket and waved an old VHS videotape in the air to emphasize his point.

"What the hell are you talking about?"

"Your every move is being recorded by the helicopter, so you might as well give it up."

"Like *hell* I will." Blood still flowed from the cuts in his knife-wielding forearm, the sting now turning into real pain.

"Hear those sirens, Skeeg? They're coming for *you*."

"Back off or I'll cut her."

Buzz ached to rush Skeeg, or pull out his gun and shoot him, but didn't dare make any sudden moves lest he startle him into using the knife. He was torn between taking action, and holding back. Then, noticing Bonnie repositioning her feet, he decided she must be preparing to go into action herself. But how? She was being firmly held with a knife to her throat. Tortured, he decided to hold himself in check a few seconds longer. He just hoped her move, whatever it was, would leave her unharmed.

An instant later, a sudden inspiration flashed through his brain. He tensed his body and leaped high into the air in an attempt to distract Skeeg. He waved his free arm and pumped his legs up and down, trying to look like a village idiot.

"*Now*, Bonnie, *now!*" he shouted.

Bonnie had prepared herself for this moment ever since Skeeg grabbed her, ever since smelling his sweaty body and his blood, ever since pretending to be completely at his mercy. Now it was time for action. Though her arms were free, she was being held tightly from behind and had a knife to her throat. Even so, she was not powerless to fight back. In a sudden move, she grabbed Skeeg's wrist with her right hand and, as she pulled it and the knife away from her throat, held on to the same wrist with her left hand. Leaning her head forward, she whipped it back, butting Skeeg in the face as hard as she could.

With his nose broken and blood gushing from his nostrils, Skeeg loosened his grip around her waist and screamed.

As soon as the knife moved away from her throat, she whirled a quarter-turn clockwise to face the arm she was holding. Then, as she pushed the knife-wielding arm downward, she crashed her right knee against its elbow, shattering it.

Skeeg dropped the knife and howled even louder.

Buzz heard the crack of the bone from twenty feet away, even above Skeeg's screams of pain and the wail of rapidly approaching sirens. Not wanting to lose control of Blackie, he had dared take only a step forward. But now, the sound of the cracking bone told him he could relax. Bonnie was in control.

Skeeg, in serious pain, and with with his right arm useless, still tried to continue the fight. Desperate, he thrust a vicious leg at Bonnie, aiming to hurt her enough to allow him to make his escape.

Bonnie, with both hands free, grabbed the extended ankle and, with a mighty tug, lifted him completely off his feet. As Skeeg fell heavily onto his back, Bonnie followed him down and jammed a knee into his groin, just as she had that night on her front lawn.

Skeeg's pain was now unbearable. With his right elbow shattered, nose broken and bleeding, and a knee grinding into his groin, Skeeg passed out without ever realizing the fight was over.

"Are you okay?" Buzz called, rushing to her

side and cuddling her as best he could with Blackie's control box still in his hand.

Bonnie removed her knee from Skeeg's damaged groin. "Yeah. I'm fine. It's *his* blood, not mine."

"Oh, yeah? Then why is that blood leaking out of your neck?"

Bonnie reached a hand to her neck to find the source of the blood.

Now that the fight was over, her hands began shaking. She leaned over to catch her breath, trying hard to control the tears streaming from her eyes.

"You've been cut. Here. Hold my hankie on it until I can find something to bandage it with."

Just then two squad cars screeched to a stop. Four police officers leaped out, guns drawn.

Arriving in response to Buzz's 911 call and seeing the front door wide open, two officers ran in to clear the house from front to back, while the other two ran directly to the yard at the rear of the house. All four reached the patio at the same time. With their guns pointed at Bonnie and Buzz, they attempted to make sense of the scene before them.

"Hands away from your body," the Sergeant commanded. They complied as best they could, what with Buzz holding the helicopter control box in one hand, and Bonnie trying to stop the trickle of blood from her neck.

"She's been cut by that bastard on the

ground," Buzz said. "She's trying to hold down the bleeding. Got a first aid kit?"

"Put that thing in your hand down. *Now*," commanded the Sergeant.

Buzz slowly squatted and placed the control box on the grass, having locked Blackie into the hover position as best he could.

"What *is* that thing, anyhow?"

"It's the remote control box for the helicopter," Buzz said, pointing to the hovering bird. "It's not a weapon."

Sensing the action was over and the danger past, the officers holstered their guns and focused their attention on the inert body on the ground.

"Okay, what happened here? We got a 911 call saying something about an armed stalker breaking into a house."

"That's him on the ground." Bonnie nodded toward the comatose Skeeg.

One of the officers knelt down for a closer look. "Jeesus. What'd you *do* to the guy?"

"Not me. *Her*." Buzz pointed to Bonnie. "I was controlling the bird. He jumped her from behind and put that knife to her throat. She taught him not to mess with a woman skilled in martial arts."

"She did that all by herself?" The officer appeared to be in awe.

"Yeah. He's damned lucky she didn't decide to finish him off in self defense."

"I ... I didn't ... have any choice," Bonnie said, still breathing heavily. "He was gonna kill me."

"Yeah?" asked a skeptical Sergeant. "How do we know it went down like you say?"

"It'll all be on the video," Buzz said.

"What video?"

"Look at the helicopter. That little lump on the underside is a camera and digital recording rig. Soon as I copy it onto a DVD, you can have it and watch the whole show."

"Well, I'll be damned!" The Sergeant, deciding Buzz's account must be the truth, pointed to one of the other officers. "Charlie, go get the first aid kit and put a bandage on the lady. And call an ambulance. *Move.*"

Charlie moved. While he ran toward the patrol cars out front, another officer ran to the house to fetch a chair for Bonnie to sit on. All four had developed a healthy respect for the lady who could pulverize a knife-wielding scumbag single-handedly.

Until now, the unconscious and bleeding lump on the ground had been totally ignored. Now, as Officer Charlie returned to apply a bandage to Bonnie's bleeding neck, Skeeg groaned in pain.

"I'll ... kill ... you ... for ... this ... bitch," he hissed, unaware that police officers stood within easy hearing distance.

"Okay," the Sergeant said. "That clinches it." Pointing to Skeeg, he said to the others, "This is the perp for sure. Soon as the ambulance gets here, cuff him to the gurney and get 'im the hell out of here."

"You got blood in your hair, lady," Officer Charlie said, brandishing the bandages. "Your head cut?"

"No, that happened when I head-butted the guy and broke his nose. I probably look a lot worse than I am," she said. "It's mostly his blood."

Bonnie began to feel somewhat recovered now that she was sitting down, but felt awkward sitting on a kitchen chair while surrounded by police officers, a helicopter hovering overhead, a groaning assailant on the ground, and Buzz kneeling beside her, stroking and kissing her hand.

During the minutes that followed, the officers worked their way through the house, making notes of the damage to the back door, the broken glass on the kitchen floor, and the trail of blood toward the bathroom and to the counter.

While Buzz and Bonnie each described their parts in the event, Charlie finished his first aid on Bonnie's neck.

After the ambulance arrived and Skeeg had been loaded onto a gurney, the police Sergeant turned to Bonnie. "You really should let us take you to the hospital for a check. It's procedure in situations like these."

"Thanks," Bonnie said, "but I don't think I'm up for it. Can't you just have one of the EMTs take a look?"

"Okay," the Sergeant said. "We really *should* take you to the hospital, but if the EMT says you're okay, we'll let it pass."

"Thank you."

"If you two can come down to the station first thing in the morning, we can get the paperwork done." He handed Bonnie his card. "Here's the address."

"We'll be there," Buzz said. He helped her stand and wrapped an arm around her. "Let's get you over to my place; you need to lie down." To the Sergeant, he said, "If you'd like to detail some-one to come next door with me, I'll make a copy of the recording right now."

"Why not just give me the one in the helicop-ter?"

"Be glad to, but you wouldn't be able to play it on your equipment. It's recorded on a pretty ad-vanced piece of hardware."

The Sergeant thought about that for two breaths. "Okay, let's do it." He issued orders to the other officers, after which the three of them trooped toward Buzz's house, Blackie leading the way a few feet above and ahead, as if proud to be a member of the team.

Chapter Twenty-Seven

"I really feel quite refreshed," Bonnie said, after a light lunch and a lengthy nap, "and I really wish you'd stop hovering around me as though I'm going to go dead any minute."

"Are you sure you're all right?" Now that Bonnie was awake, he went to the window to let the afternoon sun into the bedroom.

"Look, I appreciate your being so attentive and all, but I'm fine. Here. I'll even show you. See?" she said, lifting her left leg. "This is the knee Skeeg bashed with his groin, and it doesn't hurt a bit." She lowered the leg and raised the other. "And see this one? This is the one he bashed with his elbow, and it doesn't hurt, either. So I'm in fine shape."

"What about the cut on your neck?"

"It's practically all healed."

"Bull! Let me see it."

Bonnie pulled back the bandage the EMT had applied, and Buzz moved closer to study the wound.

"Okay. The bleeding's stopped and it doesn't

look as though it'll need stitches." He replaced the bandage. "Now, if you think you can behave your-self—"

"Whaddoyou mean by that, Birdman?"

"I mean, if you think you can lie quietly right there and rest, I'll make us some dinner."

"Under one condition."

"What's that?"

"You slather me with a few kisses ... just to help soothe my jangled nerves, you understand."

"I'll be happy to do that, provided you stay right where you are." He leaned over the bed to fulfill her request.

*   *   *

Buzz took his time preparing dinner, humming as he did. *It's kinda nice to be cooking for two,* he thought. *It'd be even nicer if it weren't just for tonight.* He'd been thinking about whether to confess his love for her, but every time he thought he'd hit on the right time and place, something unexpected interfered. *It's a helluva big step, he kept thinking. I'm not sure we know enough about each other even to think about anything permanent. Maybe she doesn't feel the same way. What if I propose and she turns me down? I think I'll just cool it until the right moment comes along.*

At that moment, Bonnie entered the dining

room. "Mmm. Smells good."

"I thought I told you to stay put."

"I needed to prepare myself for this sumptu-
ous feast. You didn't expect me to come to the table all grungy, did you?"

"Oh, all right."

"So I took a quick shower and cleaned up a little. Okay?"

Buzz took a firm, full-length look at his com-
panion. She wore a sheer three-quarter length
robe over what looked like a transparent black
nightie. "Okay, but no jumping around. Just take
a seat."

She did, and Buzz served the dinner. Salad
consisted of two slices of tomato, each dotted with
a black olive, and surrounded with thin slices of
yellow pepper. The main course, a delicate rack of
lamb, arrived accompanied by fresh asparagus and
mint jelly. When Buzz placed the serving dish on
the table, Bonnie noted he'd even gone to the trouble of making a little silver bootie for each of the
chops.

When she leaned forward for a closer look, she
broke into laughter. Actually, she howled with
laughter. After the sniffles abated enough to allow
her to speak, she said, "Do my eyes deceive me, or
are those little silvery booties actually made of
duct tape?"

Buzz arched his eyebrows and drew himself up
in imitation of a haughty butler. "They are, mad-

am, and I'll thank you not to cast asparagus on my ingenuity."

"I wouldn't think of it," Bonnie said, still snuffling between guffaws. "I was right. You *are* weird."

After dinner was consumed and the dishes cleared from the table, Buzz served some of his rich-tasting coffee, along with some of his excellent brandy.

Bonnie leaned over to reach for more.

"No, please don't get up," he said. "It's my pleasure to pamper our very own resident heroine."

"Cut the crap, peasant, and pour me another dollop. I don't ordinarily imbibe, but having just survived a trip through the valley of death, I think I'm entitled."

Buzz willingly complied. "Wouldn't you be more comfortable lying on my living room couch?"

"Looky here," Bonnie said. "All I've got is a little sore neck. The rest of me is in perfect working order. See? C'mere an' feel if you don't believe me." She pulled her thin robe to one side, revealing one of her perfectly-formed breasts. The sheer nightie might have served some cosmic purposes, but hiding her bosom from view was not one of them. She put his hand on one. "See?"

"Mmm, yes." He squeezed gently. "It seems to be in perfect working order and I definitely like what I see. By the way, is the brandy helping you relax? I think there's something I may want to ask you."

Bonnie nodded and smiled, her eyelids at half-mast, enjoying his touch as he caressed her body. "I think I can safely say that your hypothesis is correct. If I were any more relaxed I'm sure I would turn into a little puddle of protoplasm." She giggled.

"Then it's time to move to a more suitable setting. Come with me to the couch." He led his unsteady guest to the living room and settled her on the soft sofa. "Now then, since you admit to being suitably lubricated for the occasion—"

"The heck I am," she said, downing another sip. "And just what occasion are you referring to?"

"As I was trying to say, there's something I'd like to say to you."

"What?"

"You promise not to attack me?"

"I won't even kill you ... not even a little bit."

"I'm much relieved."

Buzz dropped to one knee beside her and took her hand in his.

"Bonnie, I must confess I've fallen madly in love with you, even in your soon-to-be sozzled state, and I haven't been able to think about anything but you ever since ... well, ever since. The thought of spending the rest of my life without you by my side fills me with dread and sadness."

Bonnie waggled a finger. "What makes you

think you gotta do that?"

"Do what?"

"Spend the rest of your life without me."

"Well, I—"

"Spit it out, man, spit it out. I don't think I can stay awake much longer." Eyelids drooped to underline the assertion.

"All right, I'll try." Even with Bonnie in her relaxed state, it took more courage to say the words than Buzz had expected.

"Bonnie ... will you marry me?"

"Out with it. What are you tryin' to say?"

"I just said it. I asked if you would marry me. You know, live as husband and wife, happily ever after."

"I know what you said," Bonnie said, dreamily. "Just wanted to hear you say it again." She wrapped her arms around his neck, and pulled him closer. "Be careful with my neck. It still hurts."

"Shall I say it again?"

"Say what again? Oh, that. Yeah. Say it again."

"Bonnie, I love you very much. I love every pore, every nook and cranny of your body, and every drop of blood leaking out of your neck. Will you marry me?"

"Of *course* I'll marry you ... I thought you'd never ask. Besides," she added, "I love you, too." She pulled his head to hers in an attempt to kiss

him like he'd never been kissed before. She closed
her eyes to savor the moment, but just as her lips
touched his, she emitted a long sigh of content-
ment and fell fast asleep.

*   *   *

Epilogue

Exactly ten months later, Bonnie and Buzz watched a perfect sunset from under the thatch-roofed lanai beneath which they had exchanged marriage vows less than twenty-four hours earlier. The brief ceremony, conducted by a local Japanese clergyman, had been accompanied by a ukulele playing the "Hawaiian Wedding Song."

The small wedding party, consisting of Angela and her husband, Tony, had lifted champagne glasses in tribute and congratulations to the bride and groom.

Since flying to a secluded resort on the Big Island of Hawaii three days earlier, they had adapted to relaxed "Island time." It was a perfect setting for reminiscing, honeymooning, and planning.

"This is ideal," Bonnie said, fingering the gardenia lei hanging around her neck, "and I can't tell you how much I love you."

"You could try." Buzz nuzzled her neck. "After all, you can use the practice."

"Well, *that* wasn't a point-winning comment,"

Bonnie said, knuckling him on the shoulder.

"I simply meant we'll have lots of time for re-ciprocal loving, though I'm not entirely sure you're ready for same."

Bonnie poked her chest with a finger. "Hey! *I'm* an expert."

"*Sure,* you are," Buzz teased.

"Just what do you mean by *that?*" Bonnie re-torted with mock indignation.

"As I recall, the minute I asked you to be my wife, you fell fast asleep. Is that the proper behav-ior of an expert? You showed absolutely no re-spect for the powerful effect I have on women. Ac-tually, you completely shattered my self-confidence."

"I could tell. When you tried carrying me to bed I was so limp you let me slip to the floor, after which you fell flat on your butt—"

"I did *not!* I merely slipped on a banana peel."

"Fiddleflops."

"Oh, yeah? Well, I say again—some sexpot you turned out to be. As soon as a man proposes, you take a *nap.*"

"Big surprise! You plied me with liquor."

"With what? One little sniff of brandy?"

"Never mind. You got what you deserved."

"As I recall, dear madam, *I* didn't get anything at all. Made me feel pretty silly ... not to mention frustrated."

"Silly? I'll tell you silly." Bonnie chuckled as

she recounted a portion of the "Skeeg Attack," as they had come to call it. "What was maximum silly was the sight of you, standing under Blackie, jumping up and down and waving that totally irrelevant video in your hand. What was it, anyway?"

"The video?"

"Of course, the video."

"Oh, that was our old fireplace tape. It was the first thing I could grab. I was in a hurry to rescue you, don't forget. Good thing Skeeg was too enraged to realize it was just a bluff—nobody could stuff one of those old tapes into a sleek helicopter like Blackie."

"What a loser."

"And I just loved it," Buzz continued, "when the cops came roaring in and realized you'd turned the guy into a battered lump all by your lonesome. They were impressed up to their eyeballs. Surprised they didn't get on their knees and genuflect."

"Well, they *should* have," she said. "But even funnier was when we walked into the police station the next day and found the cops sitting around watching the DVD—over and over again—"

"And they burst into applause and whistles when you walked in."

Changing the subject, Bonnie said, "You know, we never found out for sure what Skeeg was convicted of after he got out of the hospital."

"I'm not sure either—wait, here comes Tony.

He'll know."

Angela and her beloved "cop-husband," Tony, strolled toward them from the beach bar. The two had eagerly accepted Buzz's and Bonnie's invitation to take part in the ceremony.

Unfortunately, David Chin's schedule had prevented his attending; in his place, he had sent a box of books intended to add sparks to the bride and groom's wedded bliss.

"Hey there, Mr. Best Man. Wot'cha got there?" Buzz said.

"Enough truth serum to go around," Tony offered.

"You're just in time. Bonnie and I were just wondering what Skeeg was finally convicted of."

"I thought you'd never ask. He had the book thrown at him—aggravated assault with a deadly weapon, attempted kidnapping, stalking, breaking and entering, plus several other charges. He was convicted on all counts. Thanks to that DVD you managed to make, he'll be in the slammer for a long time."

"Good riddance," Buzz said. "You know, at the time, I wondered why, instead of firing him, the company hadn't simply sent Skeeg back to his sales position, since he was so good at it."

"I wondered that, too," Bonnie said, "but I learned later it was because management already had their eyes on him—Mr. Cardoza and others had been keeping a log of his missteps for almost a year. His attack on me, along with his arrest, was the final straw. That gave them the perfect opportunity to get rid of him for good. They sure didn't want a sociopath on the payroll."

"Yes," Buzz said, "and it gave them even more ammunition when the 'Bitch' file Skeeg kept on his computer listing the stalking actions he was planning somehow appeared on the computers of several Marsden executives. It really hit the fan when they realized what they were looking at. They terminated Skeeg on the spot—didn't even give him a thirty-day notice."

Tony shook his head. "Wouldn't have done him any good, what with him in the slammer. What I don't get is how they could have hired a guy like that in the first place."

"He was an excellent salesman," Bonnie said. "He could really charm the customers when it suited his purpose. But the flip side of him was something entirely different. When he was crossed," she drew a hand across her throat, "he became evil as sin. He's a sociopath; you know, a Jekyll and Hyde."

"Yeah," Tony said. "I've seen a few of those in my day. They're so slick they can be living in your neighborhood for decades without anyone becoming suspicious."

Angela added, "And if anyone doubts how dangerous they can be, just Google 'sociopath.' You'll get the full grisly story."

"There's only one thing that puzzles me," Tony said, turning toward Bonnie. "If I remember right, Buzz proposed about a year ago and—"

"Yup," Buzz said, "and a minute after she said 'yes' she promptly fell asleep."

Bonnie, pretending pique, said, "Yes, and if you don't forget about that pretty soon we can be *unmarried* just as promptly."

"What I was trying to ask," Tony said, "is why it took you two so long to get married after she accepted your proposal."

"We tried," Buzz said. "But every time we thought we had enough free days lined up at the same time, something always interfered. And, as soon as the papers published Blackie's pictures of a demolished Skeeg lying crumpled on the ground, Bonnie's already-busy consulting business skyrocketed. Now that she's a celebrity, it seems like she's always off to the other end of the planet."

"And hubby here," Bonnie added, "still flits about to attend meetings, and work on hush-hush projects. So it took a long time to make our calendars behave, but at last we managed and here we are."

"Now that you two are safely married off, what's next?" Angela asked.

"Well," Buzz replied, "that's going to be a little tough, at least for awhile. Next week, Bonnie's leaving for Hong Kong to work with new clients, and I'm off to spend a couple of weeks at the Pentagon."

"So," Bonnie added, "we still don't have enough time together to get this marriage off the ground. But as soon as I return from Asia, I'll get started on the next big project."

"Oh?" Buzz asked. "What project?"

"Us."

"*Us?*"

"Yes, us. We've always been a couple of independent loners, you know. It's going to take some real work to weld ourselves into a working team. First, I'll have to clear out that messy basement of yours and put up some nice curtains and flowers, and then get you shaped into a doting husband—"

"Hey," Buzz protested, his fingers flicking champagne in her direction.

"Just kidding." Bonnie smiled, wiping her face. "I wouldn't change a thing ... Mister Downstairs Slob."

Buzz swatted Bonnie playfully on her behind. "Talk like that will net you a serious spanking ... and you know what that means. Hmm. Come to think of it, this seems like a good time to put that thought into action."

Taking her by the hand, he pulled her to a vertical position, slipped an arm around her waist, and guided her toward their thatched honeymoon cottage.

*   *   *

Made in the USA
Charleston, SC
24 December 2011